"You've grown up, Gem."

Tears welled in Gemma's throat, making it hard to reply. "What—what did you expect?"

"Oh, I expected something quite spectacular." The skin around Max's eyes creased as he smiled.

This conversation was dangerous, but she was mesmerized by his voice—deep, yet rough around the edges, as if his throat felt as choked as hers. She couldn't drag herself away, despite the embarrassing memories still hot in her thoughts.

As if sensing her confusion, Max took both her hands in his and pulled her toward him. "Now that you're so grown up, I think it's time we talked about a little matter that we should have discussed long ago—five years ago."

OUTBACK BABY
Barbara Hannay

TORONTO • NEW YORK • LONDON
AMSTERDAM • PARIS • SYDNEY • HAMBURG
STOCKHOLM • ATHENS • TOKYO • MILAN • MADRID
PRAGUE • WARSAW • BUDAPEST • AUCKLAND

For Lucy Francesca, who was born into our family
at the time this story was coming to life.

ISBN 0-373-03690-6

OUTBACK BABY

First North American Publication 2002.

Copyright © 2000 by Barbara Hannay.

CHAPTER ONE

WHEN Gemma heard the pounding on her front door, she knew something was desperately wrong. Startled, she hurried to answer it, hardly expecting to find her best friend on her doorstep, clutching her ten-month-old daughter to her chest as if the baby were a life-preserver.

'I need your help, Gemma. Are you terribly busy?'

Shocked by the fear in her friend's eyes, Gemma slipped a reassuring arm around her shoulders. 'Bel, you know I'm never too busy for you. Come in and tell me what's wrong.'

Isobel stepped into the flat with a shaky sigh and hefted baby Mollie higher on her hip. Her eyes darted to the pile of paperwork on Gemma's dining table. 'Oh, you *are* busy. I'm sorry.'

'Don't worry about this mess.' With a quick dismissive gesture, Gemma gathered up the designs she'd just finished and slipped them into a manila folder. For the moment she would have to put aside her own panic about deadlines and the need to dash this marketing brochure to the printers this afternoon. Isobel was obviously besieged by much more serious problems. 'How can I help?'

To Gemma's horror, Isobel's normally serene face crumpled and tears spilled onto her cheeks. 'It's Dave.'

'Dave? Has something happened in Africa?' Two months earlier, Isobel's husband Dave had been seconded by an Australian aid agency to sink wells in Somalia.

Isobel hugged Mollie even closer and rested a trembling chin on the baby's curly head. 'It's so sudden, it's terrible. He's being held hostage. I'm sure it's all some awful mistake, but rebels are involved.' She drew a deep shuddering breath, clearly trying to suppress the urge to burst into full-scale crying.

'I can't believe it,' Gemma whispered, gripping her friend's cold fingers while she gaped at her.

Surely this sort of thing didn't happen to ordinary people? Not to easygoing, cheerful Dave Jardine?

She groped for the right words and gave up the struggle. 'I'm so sorry. This is terrible. Poor Dave.' The thought of her childhood friend—the boy she'd grown up with in the bush—facing armed rebels was appalling. How could his wife bear it? She stared helplessly at Isobel's white face and whispered, 'What can we do?'

'I'm going to him,' Isobel answered with a determined lift of her chin.

'*You're* going to Africa?' Gemma pulled out another chair and sat down swiftly. This second shock was almost worse than the first. 'What can you do?' she asked at last.

'Apparently I'm the only one who can do anything,' Isobel explained with wide, frightened eyes. 'Because I'm Dave's wife, the people at the Australian Embassy think I can help. Dave's there for humanitarian reasons and they think the rebels are more likely to respond if we work on the family angle.'

'Oh, Isobel, how brave of you!!' Gemma jumped up again and hugged her. 'Lucky Dave to have such a wonderful wife.' She smiled wistfully. 'Love and the kind of marriage that you guys have—it's—it's *amazing*!' For Gemma it was beyond imagining. With a short burst of pride, she remembered that she shared responsibility for this wonderful partnership by introducing Isobel and Dave during their university days.

Her gaze dropped to the innocent baby perched happily on her mother's lap. 'You couldn't dream of taking little Mollie into a dangerous situation like that?'

'No, of course I couldn't.' Isobel sighed and pressed her lips to her daughter's chubby cheek. 'I can't bear the thought of leaving her behind, but that's where you come in, Gem. I've an enormous favour to ask.'

'Of course—I'll do anything.' Gemma did her best to ignore the nervous knot tightening in her stomach as her mind raced.

'I'm sorry I didn't ring you first to warn you, but I knew you were going to be home and...' Isobel's voice trailed away as she looked at her friend hopefully.

'Just tell me how I can help.'

'I was hoping you could mind Mollie for me.'

Gemma gulped. While she adored Mollie, she knew absolutely zilch about caring for babies. She pressed her lips tightly together before she verbalised any of the sudden doubts that swamped her. Of course she could mind a baby. Millions of women all over the world had been doing it for centuries without turning a hair. 'I'd love to have her,' she said with a bright smile.

Isobel reached out and squeezed Gemma's hand. 'I'm sorry I've dumped this on you at such short notice, but I wouldn't trust anyone else to look after my little girl. My parents are on holiday in Spain, as you know. Dave's father is too old—and it has to be someone I know well. Someone who cares about Mollie. Not a nanny I've never met. Honestly, Gem, you're my best friend and, working from home as you do, I couldn't think of anyone better.'

'I'm flattered that you trust me,' Gemma responded

warmly, but she couldn't help adding, 'You do realise, don't you, that I—I don't have much experience with babies. Actually—I don't have *any* experience with them.'

'Oh, Gemma, you've been around Mollie heaps. And you'll be amazed how it all comes so instinctively. I'm sure you're a natural!' She gave her daughter a motherly hug. 'And Mollie's really quite a good little poppet.'

'Of course,' Gemma responded quickly, not wanting to alarm her friend. 'She's a darling.' When she thought about Dave's desperate plight and Isobel's brave decision to go to Africa, Gemma knew she could hardly make a fuss about caring for one perfectly harmless and tiny human being.

Her friend's grey eyes brightened. 'Don't worry,' she said, 'I've rung Max. I'm sure he'll be happy to help you any way he can.'

'Max?' Gemma had been playing with Mollie's pink toes, but at the mention of Dave's older brother Max, her head jerked up. 'I won't need any help from *him!*'

To her annoyance, Gemma's heart began a fretful pounding.

Since she'd been six years old, Max Jardine had always managed to get under her skin. When they were teenagers, Gemma had never been able to understand why the girls in the outback town of Goodbye Creek, where she and the Jardine boys had gone to school, had scored Max a 'hunk factor' of ten. They had raved about his well-toned body and dark good looks.

'But you've seriously overlooked his personality defects,' she'd pointed out.

'What defects?' the girls had scoffed.

And Gemma had rolled her eyes in disgust. She was well-acquainted with his faults. She'd spent half her childhood on the Jardine's property, camping and canoeing or horse-riding with Dave, and Max had always been in the background, treating her like a bad smell that hung around his brother.

In the years since she'd left the outback she'd only seen Max a handful of times, but nothing had changed. He still looked on her as a lower life-form. She shook her head. 'Max Jardine would know even less than I do about caring for a baby.'

Isobel was regarding Gemma strangely. 'I didn't realise you were so touchy about Max.'

'I'm not *touchy* about him,' Gemma snapped.

Isobel's eyebrows rose. 'If you say so.'

'It's just that I fail to see how a man who spends his whole life marooned in the outback like a hermit with only cattle for company could be any use when it comes to minding Mollie.'

'Maybe you're right,' Isobel agreed cautiously. 'But let's not forget that Max *is* Dave's brother. I had to let him know what had happened.'

Gemma could hardly deny that, but it didn't help her to feel any better. 'How did he react?' she asked warily.

'Actually, I couldn't speak to him directly. There was no answer when I rang through to the property this morning, so I left a message on his answering machine. He must be out in the bush mustering or maybe fencing, so I simply explained what I was going to do.'

'And you told him I would be taking care of Mollie?'

'I said that was my plan.'

'I see.'

Gemma decided there and then that if Max Jardine knew she'd been asked to care for Mollie, she would mind this baby as expertly as a triple-certificated nanny. This wasn't just a case of helping out her best friend.

She didn't want to give Mollie's grumpy Uncle Max one tiny chance to criticise her.

Exactly why Gemma cared about Max's opinion was an issue she didn't have time to consider now. She was too busy worrying about how she could mind Mollie *and* carry on her business.

But she would find a way. She might collapse in the attempt, but she would give it her best shot.

Lifting Mollie from Isobel's arms, Gemma cuddled her close. The baby girl was soft and warm and smelt delicious. 'Tell me everything I need to know about our little darling.'

'Oh, Gem. I'm so relieved. I knew I could depend on you.' Isobel let out a relieved sigh. 'I can give you everything you'll need for Mollie. In fact, my bag's packed and I have it all in the car.'

'You mean you're heading off today?'

'It's important that I get to Dave as fast as I can. I'll get Mollie's things for you now.'

'Sure,' Gemma replied, more confidently than she felt. 'You get the baby gear and I'll make us some coffee.'

By the time she'd drunk her coffee, Gemma's mind was reeling. She had three closely written pages of detailed instructions about caring for Mollie. At the outset, Isobel had said minding a baby was simple, but Mollie came with more operating instructions than a state-of-the-art computer.

How could one little scrap require so much work? And how, she wondered, after she'd waved goodbye to Isobel, could she suddenly manage Mollie and her business? She looked at the pink and white bundle in her arms and tried to suppress a surge of alarm. She had immediate deadlines to meet and there was the constant need to drum up new clients.

Mollie's round little eyes stared solemnly up at her, reminding Gemma of an unblinking owl. Her heart melted. 'Kiddo, it's just you and me now. And we're not going to let this lick us.' She dropped a quick kiss on Mollie's curly head. Then she walked briskly back up the path to her flat, determined to tackle this task in as businesslike a fashion as possible.

A swish of tyres behind her brought her spinning around. In her driveway, a taxi was pulling up and a tall, rangy figure leapt from the passenger's seat.

Max Jardine!

How in tarnation had he got from Western Queensland to Brisbane so quickly?

'Gemma!' Max barked as he swung open her front gate and strode towards her. His piercing blue eyes were fixed on Mollie. 'Where's Isobel?'

'Hello, Max. Nice to see you, too,' Gemma replied coolly while her heart thudded. Max switched his gaze to her and he glared as ferociously as a headmaster scowling at an unmanageable pupil. Suddenly, she felt extremely self-conscious—as if her skirt was too short, her black stockings too sheer, or her platform heels too high. No matter how much decorum she'd acquired over the years, this older brother of Dave's always, always, *always* made her feel like a silly little girl. 'How did you get here so quickly?' she demanded.

'I flew. I got in early this morning from checking out the back country and found Isobel's message on the answering machine.'

Gemma remembered that she'd been told Max had invested in his own light aircraft.

'Well, Isobel's already left for Eagle Farm airport. You probably passed her.'

Max grimaced. 'So she's going ahead with this madcap scheme?'

'Yes, she's a very determined woman.' Gemma hugged Mollie a little closer. Faced by this angry maelstrom of a man, she found the baby's warmth and softness reassuring.

Cursing, Max ran impatient fingers through his dark brown hair. 'I should be the one chasing across the world after Dave.'

Gemma smacked a hand to her forehead, pantomime-style, and beamed at him. 'What a brilliant idea! Why didn't Isobel or I think of that? You're the obvious choice. You're Dave's brother. You're family but, even better, you're a man. You could spare Isobel the danger and Isobel—' Gemma felt a heady rush of excitement and relief as the next point sank in '—and Isobel could continue to care for Mollie.'

'So you don't want to look after the baby?'

'I—I didn't say that.' Her sense of relief plummeted. She and Max had hardly been talking for thirty seconds and already he'd found a way to put her down. 'Of course I'm happy to mind her, but could you really go to Africa? Do you have your passport with you?'

'Don't you think I haven't tried to go?' Max glared back at her. 'Foreign Affairs quickly knocked me back. They told me in no uncertain terms to stay out of it. Isobel is Dave's next of kin and they want the wifely touch to try to appeal on humanitarian grounds. Apparently, that's much more likely to get Dave released. I'm not happy, but I'm not going to muddy the water.'

Gemma's shoulders sagged. 'I suppose that's wise. It does sound like a touchy situation.'

Max merely grunted. He moved up the path towards

her and she found herself backing away from his deter-mined stride. Some women had been heard to comment that now he'd reached thirty Max was even more good-looking than he'd been in his teens, but none of them had enticed him into marriage and Gemma knew why. His personality hadn't improved one jot.

'Who decided that you should be taking care of the baby?' he drawled.

She squared her shoulders. 'Her mother is absolutely certain that I am the perfect choice.'

A sudden wind gusted across the garden and Gemma ducked her head to protect Mollie, so she missed seeing his reaction. But she didn't miss the sound of her front door slamming shut. Horrified, she whirled around. *Dammit!* Now she was stranded on her own front path with a baby in her arms and Max Jardine glowering at her.

He looked in the direction of her door. 'You're not locked out, are you?'

She fumbled around in her pockets, knowing that it was useless and that her keys were still hanging on a little brass hook in her kitchen. 'Yes,' she replied through gritted teeth.

'You can't get in the back way?'

'No. I made sure I closed my back door because I was worried about my neighbour's cat and…the baby.'

For a fraction of a second, she almost thought he smiled at her. 'So it's a case of climbing through a win-dow.'

Gemma looked at her windows. It had been windy all day and the only one she'd left open was in her bed-room.

'I can get through there in a flash,' Max offered.

She pictured him swinging his riding boots and his

long, jeans-clad legs over the sill, squeezing past the big
bed that almost filled her small room—seeing the mud-
dle of books, perfume and make-up on her bedside table
and the underwear she'd left in a jumble on the end of
the bed.

For some silly reason, she felt ridiculously flustered
at the mere thought of Max seeing her private domain.
'It's OK,' she said quickly. 'I'll go. I—I know my way
around.'

This time he was definitely smiling. His blue eyes
danced as they rested first on Mollie in her arms and
then on her short skirt. 'If you insist on getting in there
yourself, let me at least help.' He held out his arms for
Mollie.

Oh, Lord! What was worse? Did she want Max
Jardine prowling around her bedroom, or Max, with
Mollie in one arm, helping her up to her window and
watching her skirt hike over her hips as she clambered
through? Damn the man! Why did his presence always
rock her so badly? This was hardly a life-threatening
situation and yet she was feeling completely rattled.

'I guess you've got the longer legs. You'd better do
the climbing,' she muttered ungraciously.

'OK,' he agreed easily, and in no time he had disappeared.

She saw her lace curtain snag as Max moved past it
and she wondered what he thought of the ridiculously
huge bed that dominated her tiny bedroom. She had
taken the flat because it came fully furnished and the
rent was cheap, considering how closely it was situated
to the central business district. Most tenants, she assumed, would consider the king-size bed a bonus, but it
was rather more than she needed.

The front door swung open.

'Miss Brown, Miss Mollie,' Max welcomed them with a deep bow.

'Thanks,' Gemma replied stiffly as she sailed past him into her flat with her head high. At the entrance to her lounge room, she paused and eyed him coolly, feeling uncomfortably more like the guest than the hostess. To right matters she added, 'I take it you've come to visit us?'

'We've got to work out what's best for this little one.'

Gemma sighed. She sensed combat ahead of her and here she was, facing the enemy without any time to construct a battle plan. The whole business of getting into the flat had set her off on the wrong foot. 'Isobel has already decided what's best for her daughter,' she told him haughtily. 'Don't forget this baby's mother is my best friend.'

'And this baby is my niece,' Max growled.

What would poor little Mollie think, if she could understand the way they were bickering over her?

Max moved away and she grimaced as he surveyed her lounge room. Its appearance had deteriorated somewhat now that Mollie's gear was piled in the middle of the carpet. Out of the corner of her eye, she noted Max's brows pull into a frown as he studied the mountain of equipment. There were numerous toys, a collapsible cot, a car seat, pram and playpen, not to mention enough clothes to dress an entire kindergarten.

His gaze also took in the piles of pamphlets and boxes Gemma had 'filed' on her sofa. Her computer and more paperwork covered the small dining table.

'There'll be much more room when I move the baby's gear into the bedroom,' she explained hastily.

Max cracked half a grin. 'Which bedroom would that be?'

'M-mine.'

'How many bedrooms do you have?'

Why her cheeks should flame at such a straightforward question was beyond her. 'Just—just the one,' she stammered.

Max stood staring at her with his hands on his hips, shaking his head as if he hadn't heard her properly. 'You're going to put all this gear in that miniature bedroom I just came through?'

'Some of it,' she mumbled.

'You'll need to buy a smaller bed.'

Gemma wouldn't give into his provocation by responding to that comment. To her further annoyance, he turned and sauntered around her compact kitchen, then back to the lounge and dining area, silently, grimly inspecting every detail. Her dwelling seemed smaller than ever with his large frame invading the space. Finally, he swivelled back to face her. And for an unnecessarily long moment, his disturbing blue eyes rested on her.

At last he spoke very quietly. 'It can't be done, Gemma. You can't take care of Mollie here in this shoebox.'

'Of course I can. Isobel has total faith in me.'

'Isobel is desperate.'

Gemma told herself she should expect a hurtful jab like this from Max and she resolved not to let him intimidate her. She matched his challenging gaze with a scornful glare. 'Isobel wasn't so desperate that she'd risk her baby's welfare. She has complete trust in my ability to care for Mollie.'

His eyes narrowed as he stared thoughtfully at the toes of his leather riding boots.

'Why don't you?' she challenged.

His head came up slowly, but he didn't speak.

'Why don't you trust me, Max?'

Before he replied, he thrust his hands deep into the pockets of his faded jeans. 'I'm sure you have good intentions, Gemma. But I keep remembering…' His Adam's apple moved up and down rapidly.

When he paused, Gemma rushed to defend herself. 'I doubt that you've noticed, but I'm not a little kid any more.'

This time his mouth curved into a relaxed smile and his amused blue gaze rested on her for an uncomfortable length of time before he spoke. 'Believe me, kiddo, I've noticed how grown-up you look these days.'

No amount of willpower could prevent Gemma's blushes. She ducked her face behind Mollie's golden curls.

'But what I'm remembering is your reaction at the hospital when Mollie was born,' he continued. 'You told us all very loudly that you were allergic to babies. You wouldn't touch her for fear she would break.'

Gemma tried valiantly to suppress a gasp of dismay. 'Newborn babies don't count,' she muttered defensively. 'Everyone's nervous about holding them. I love Mollie now.'

'But you said you were going to wait till she was old enough to—what was it? Take shopping? I think you were planning to teach her how to buy shoes and where to get the very best coffee in town.'

Stunned, Gemma stared at Max. The man had the memory of an elephant! She had only dim recollections of this conversation. How on earth did he retain such insignificant details? He must make a habit of hoarding up ammunition like this to fire when it most hurt.

'OK, I was scared of Mollie at first,' she admitted. 'I'd never been in close contact with such a tiny new baby before, but I—I've adjusted. Mollie and I get on famously now.'

At that moment, Mollie wriggled restlessly in Gemma's arms and uttered a little cry of protest. Gemma stared helplessly at the squirming baby. *Just whose side was this kid on?* She tried to jiggle Mollie on her hip. She'd seen Isobel do it many times and it always seemed to work.

'I take it,' added Max, 'you're going to *try* to play nursemaid and carry on a business as well?'

'Of course. It shouldn't be a problem.' It was the worst possible moment for Mollie to let out an ear-splitting wail, but she did. Her little face turned deep pink, her bottom lip wobbled and she sobbed desperately. Feeling totally threatened, Gemma quickly placed the baby on the floor at her feet. To her surprise, Mollie stopped crying almost immediately. She sat there quietly and began to suck her fist.

'Look at that,' Gemma beamed, feeling a whole lot better. 'I won't have to cart her around every minute of the day. I'll be able to sit her in her playpen surrounded by toys and get on with my work.'

Max's expression softened for a moment as he watched his niece, but when his gaze reached Gemma again, he scowled, shook his head and shoved his hands deeper in the pockets of his jeans. 'I'm not going to allow her to stay here, Gemma.'

'I beg your pardon?' *Not going to allow her? Could she be hearing this?* Gemma had always wondered what people meant when they described hackles rising on the backs of their necks. Now she knew.

'You heard me. I'm not going to abandon my niece.'

'*Abandon* her?' she echoed. 'How dare you insinuate that leaving her with me is the same as abandoning her?'

'Don't take it personally, Gem.'

The relaxed way Max leaned back against her kitchen bench doubled Gemma's anger.

'How on earth am I supposed to take it?'

'This is a family matter. You know the old saying about blood being thicker than water. A friend can't be expected to take on such responsibility.'

'For crying out loud, I'm more than a friend,' Gemma cried. 'I'm Mollie's godmother!' But as the words left her lips, she realised they weren't much help. This man, this enemy, this ogre—was poor Mollie's godfather.

'How on earth are *you* going to look after Mollie?' Gemma challenged before Max could respond. 'You've no women on your property and only a handful of ringers. I doubt they'll be much help.'

'I'll hire a nanny, of course. Someone with the very best training.'

She made an exaggerated show of rolling her eyes in disgust. 'If Isobel wanted a nanny for Mollie, she could have hired one herself. The poor woman doesn't know how long she's going to be away and she wants someone she knows, someone who really cares about her baby, not a stranger who happens to have official qualifications.'

Max sighed and ran long fingers through his hair as he stared at the waxed tiles on Gemma's kitchen floor. 'Isobel said she didn't want a nanny?'

'Yes,' she replied firmly.

'OK,' he said at last. With another deeper sigh, his head flicked sideways and his eyes locked onto hers. 'You and I are both Mollie's godparents, so we should make this a shared responsibility.'

CHAPTER TWO

'WHAT exactly do you mean?' Gemma asked, appalled by what Max seemed to be suggesting.

'We're both the baby's godparents. So we look after her.' His eyes revealed the briefest twinkle. *'Together.'*

She knew her mouth was gaping. 'You and me?' she gasped.

'Yeah.'

'But we can't.'

'Why not?'

'It—it's not necessary. Being a godparent is simply a gesture of intent.'

Resting his hands on the counter top, Max leaned forward. 'You can't have it both ways, Gemma. Either being Mollie's godmother is a good reason for you to take care of her, or it isn't.'

She knew she was losing ground fast. Apparently Max had been honing his skills as a bush lawyer. She ran frantic fingers through her short, dark hair. 'But it doesn't mean we're obliged to— For crying out loud, Max, that doesn't mean we have to actually do anything *parental* together.'

Max's eyes teased her. 'It's the only sensible solution. You and Mollie should come and stay on Goodbye Creek Station until Isobel returns. That way we can share the load. It's called co-operation.'

Her stomach lurched as if she were coming down in a very fast elevator. 'Co-operation, my foot!' she said at last. 'How much co-operation are *you* planning to contribute? I'm the one who'll have to make all the sacrifices. Why should *I* give up everything here to head off into the bush and stay with you?'

'Because, as I've already explained,' Max said, with exaggerated patience, 'we need to share this responsibility. That way we can both get on with our work commitments.' He pointed to the pamphlets and papers on her sofa. 'I imagine it will be much easier for you to bring your stuff to Goodbye Creek and to carry on your business from there, than for me to bring thousands of head of cattle down to this, er—cosy little suburban flat.'

He was so smug and sure of himself, Gemma wanted to thump him. She was beginning to feel cornered. 'It won't work.'

'I think it's a compromise that has distinct possibilities.'

If only she could tell him she was far too busy— booked up to organise half a dozen events—but even if she did tell such a lie, she was sure he would find a way to use it against her. Instead she glared at him. 'We'll spend the whole time fighting!'

He pretended to be shocked by her words. 'Why on earth should we do that?'

Gemma groaned. '*Maxwell T.* Jardine, I don't believe I'm hearing this. We would fight, for the simple reason that we have never agreed about anything. Haven't you noticed the only thing we have in common is that we both breathe oxygen? We can't stand each other!'

Just to prove how utterly detestable he was, Max burst out laughing.

Gemma gave in to her anger. She smashed her fist onto the counter. 'What's so funny?' she yelled.

'Oh, Gemma,' he chuckled. 'You certainly are all grown up now, aren't you?'

Choking, she gasped and spluttered. Trust Max to point out that she wasn't nearly as sophisticated and worldly wise as she liked to think she was. She had a sneaking suspicion that she might never become mature and discerning. It was her long-term ambition to become cool and detached—especially when this man was around doing his best to flummox her.

For a brief moment, Max's expression softened. Then he stepped around the counter and towards her. Gemma wished he wouldn't. When he rested his strong, warm hands on both her shoulders, her nerves were way too strained to cope.

'*Gemma Elizabeth* Brown,' he said, his voice low and gravelly.

Her eyes widened at his use of her middle name. She hadn't even realised he knew it.

'We agree on the most important thing.'

She could feel the heat of his hands as they held her. Her lungs appeared to be malfunctioning, but Max didn't notice, he just kept on talking.

'We agree that Mollie deserves very good care and, on this occasion, I think most definitely, we *do* have to do something together.' His eyes flashed as he added, 'Something *parental*. You're right, we'll probably fight like cats and dogs, but we'll manage somehow—for Mollie's sake. On our own, we'd both have major difficulties looking after the poor little kid properly, wouldn't we?'

She allowed her gaze to meet those deep blue eyes, those disturbing blue eyes, and Gemma felt less sure of her line of argument.

'Together, we stand a fair chance of success—both for Mollie and our work.'

What he proposed was unthinkable! She couldn't let

this happen. How on earth could she live with Max while he inspected her babysitting skills? She'd be a dithering mess. Holy smoke, he'd be checking up on her every minute of the day and he would soon discover she knew absolutely zero about babies.

Gemma felt as if she'd stepped aside and become a spectator of this discussion. Incredibly, she realised she was nodding, accepting Max's terms.

If only she could remember exactly when Max had turned their battle to his advantage, but she had loosened her grip on this whole scene. She'd lost sight of her counter-argument.

'I'll do my fair share,' Max added. 'I'll give Mollie her tucker or bathe her, or whatever's necessary. We can work out some sort of roster if you like.'

She passed a dazed hand across her eyes. Never in her wildest dreams had she pictured this rough-riding cattleman in a hands-on relationship with a baby. She tried to visualise him attending to Mollie, but her musings were interrupted by the telephone.

'Oh, heavens! That's probably the printers.' Gemma had almost forgotten her current project and her deadline this afternoon. 'I have to get some pamphlet designs to them before five o'clock.' She glared fiercely at Max as she hurried to the phone.

'Hello, Gemma Brown speaking.'

A woman's voice reached her. 'Gemma, Sue Easton from Over the Page. I was wondering…'

The printers were chasing her copy. Gemma reassured the woman that everything was ready and she would be at their office shortly. As she spoke, she heard Mollie begin to cry behind her and she was acutely aware of Max moving quietly in the flat.

Mollie's wails ceased abruptly and by the time

Gemma put the receiver down and turned to face Max again, she was startled to find him perched on the arm of her sofa and jogging the delighted baby on his knee.

He looked very pleased with himself. 'See? You can't manage without me, can you? I'll mind this little possum while you do whatever running around you need to this afternoon.'

'Thanks,' she replied uncertainly.

'And after that,' he said with confident assurance, 'we can plan your move to Goodbye Creek. I'll book into a pub tonight and we can head off first thing in the morning.'

As he continued to favour both Gemma and Mollie with a look of smug satisfaction, the baby's face turned red and Gemma noticed that she seemed to be concentrating very hard.

'Oh-oh.' Max's confident grin slipped. Cautiously, he lifted Mollie away from his knee.

'Has she dirtied her nappy?' asked Gemma.

'I—I think so.'

At the sight of his sudden dismay, Gemma felt an urge to grin, but she managed to keep a straight face. 'Thanks so much, Max. It would be great if you could watch Mollie for half an hour or so. I do have several errands to run—especially if I'm moving house. Let me show you where the clean nappies are...' She rummaged in the pile of things Isobel had left and produced a freshly folded nappy and a container of baby wipes and, with a deadpan expression, handed them to him. 'These are what you need.'

'You're running out on me at a moment like this?' he asked, clearly horrified. By now he was holding Mollie at arm's length.

'I'm sorry,' Gemma murmured sweetly, 'but I really

do have important deadlines to meet. You'll be fine.' She gathered up her designs and her handbag and rushed out her front door.

'He thinks he's such a hotshot babysitter, he can manage this one,' she muttered under her breath.

But she wished she didn't feel quite so guilty about deserting him.

The next day, when Max piloted their plane over the vast property that made up Goodbye Creek Station, Gemma was stunned by the unexpected flood of homesickness that swept through her. It was five years since she'd been back, but she knew the Jardine family holding almost as well as she knew the township of Goodbye Creek, where her own home had been. Her parents had owned a stock and station agency in the town. They had sold up and moved to the coast about the same time she'd gone away to university.

Now, she and Max were flying back, the plane stacked carefully with the baby's gear. Max explained that he had a well-equipped study complete with an up-to-the-minute computer and a fax machine, so Gemma only needed to bring her clothes, a box of computer disks and her paperwork.

They'd left Brisbane just as dawn broke and during the five-hour flight Mollie had alternated between napping and waking for little snacks and drinks. Gemma had kept her entertained with picture books and games of 'This little pig went to market'.

Max had chatted very politely about the weather and the scenery beneath them, but it occurred to Gemma that he was behaving more like a newly introduced acquaintance than someone who had known her for more than twenty years. But now, as heart-wrenchingly familiar red soil plains unfolded below, she felt edgy, knowing that once they landed their shared past could no longer be ignored.

Wriggling forward in her seat, she peered eagerly through the windscreen, wondering why the sight of dry, grassy paddocks and straggly stands of eucalypts should make her feel so soppy and sentimental. Way below, she could recognise the signs of spring merging into summer. Early wet season storms had brought bright green new growth and purple and yellow wild flowers were poking up through the grass.

Max's flight-path followed the course of the old creek that had given its name to the district and Gemma noted that water was already flowing down its entire length. She could make out the shallow, rocky stretch of rapids and finally the deeper section they called Big Bend.

Fringed by majestic paperbarks, this cool, shady pool had been a favourite spot for childhood picnics. At the age of ten, Gemma had rocketed in a tractor tube right through the rapids as far as the Big Bend. She'd been so proud of herself and Dave had been lavish with his praise.

'You're as good as a boy,' he'd shouted. 'You made it the whole way without squealing once. Max, isn't she great?'

But Max, of course, had merely grunted and looked bored.

As they neared the homestead, her sense of nostalgia increased.

'Nearly home,' said Max, with a contented little smile, as he worked the controls to increase their angle of descent.

First came the stockyards and the corrugated iron roofs under which hay bales would be stacked to protect them from the rain. Then she could see the smaller, original holding yard, made of old timbers weathered to a silvery grey and built in the rustic post and rail design that had been around since the pioneering days.

Gemma glanced at Mollie dozing in her little safety seat beside her. 'Has Mollie been out here before?' she asked.

'No,' admitted Max. 'This will be the first time she's set foot on Jardine soil. It's a significant moment.' He made a sweeping gesture with his arm. 'All this is her inheritance.'

'Unless you have children of your own,' Gemma said softly. 'I guess then they would all be shareholders.'

He turned and their eyes met. His blue gaze held a disquieting mixture of uncertainty and bitterness. 'Yeah,' he said, and then jerked his head back to the front. 'There's always that possibility.'

They swooped a little lower and the familiar sight of the muddy dam dotted with black ducks and the rusty metal skeleton of the old windmill standing sentry nearby made her feel ridiculously emotional. She blinked her eyes to clear the misted view. In her imagination, she could hear the squeak and clank of the old windmill as it slowly pumped water to the drinking troughs.

Within seconds she was exclaiming. 'Max, my goodness! You've installed a satellite dish.'

'Got to keep up with technology.'

Their plane continued its descent and he nodded to their right, past the machinery sheds and workshops. 'I've put in some new windmills, too. That one over there has a solar panel and an electric pump.'

'Is it better than the old one?' she asked, doubtfully eyeing the shiny modern equipment.

'Too right. Before, it was always a case of no breeze, no water. Now we can get a constant flow if we need it.'

But the biggest surprise came as they made the final dip towards the airstrip, when Gemma saw the homestead, which for as long as she could remember had been a comfortable but shabby timber home with peeling paint and vine-covered wrap-around verandahs.

'Wow!' Her breath exhaled slowly as she absorbed the changes. Max's home was now a showplace. 'What have you done to the house?' she asked.

He was concentrating on making an initial swoop over the strip to clear the ground of horses and birds before attempting a landing. 'Painted it,' he muttered tersely as he swung the plane around to double back for the approach.

Below them, skittish horses cantered out of their way and a flock of cockatoos, feeding on grass seed, lifted their wings to disperse like so many pieces of white paper caught in a wind gust. The plane plunged lower and finally touched down on the gravel runway.

'What a difference,' Gemma exclaimed, still staring at Max's house, amazed by the transformation. The homestead's timber walls were now painted a pretty powder blue, the iron roof was a clean, crisp silver and all the trims and the lattice on the verandahs were gleaming white.

As they taxied down the short airstrip, Max shot her a cautious glance. 'You like it?'

'It's beautiful, Max. I had no idea the old place could look so lovely.' She was startled to see an unexpected red tinge creep along his cheekbones. 'Who did the job for you?'

'Did it myself,' he muttered. 'During the dry season, of course.'

Another shock.

As the plane came to a standstill, Gemma assimilated this news and sat quietly, thinking about the lonely weeks Max must have spent on the task. The life of an outback cattleman was solitary and hard and the men who survived it were tough, complex creatures. And they didn't come much more complicated than Max, she thought with a wry grimace. 'It's fantastic,' she told him with genuine warmth. 'You've done an amazing job.'

He looked embarrassed and she realised he was probably more used to her scorn than her praise. She allowed herself a private smile as she thought about that. They were probably both much more comfortable fighting than co-operating.

An old utility truck had been left at the end of the runway and Gemma and Max were kept busy for the next ten minutes, transferring Mollie and the gear into the vehicle. Even though it was only a few hundred metres to the homestead, there was too much to lug such a distance.

It was late morning. The sun was already high overhead and very hot and so, by the time they reached the kitchen, a cool drink was the first priority. Gemma found Mollie's little feeding cup, while Max swung his fridge door open and grabbed a jug of iced water.

Just before he closed the fridge, he paused to survey its contents and frowned. 'I might have to stock up on a few things from town,' he commented before filling a glass and handing it to Gemma. 'I'm afraid I wasn't expecting you and I haven't got the kind of fancy things that women like for breakfast. I'm still a steak and eggs man myself.'

Gemma's eyes widened. 'How do you know what women like for breakfast?' The question was out before she really thought through what she was saying. She'd always pictured Max as a crusty bachelor living the life of a lonely recluse in the back of beyond.

Max went very still and she cringed with sudden shame as she recognised just how rude and downright stupid her query sounded. How on earth could she retract her words?

Before any bright ideas struck, he spun around, and the glance he sent her way was tinged with wry amusement.

Had she left her brains in Brisbane? Of course this man would have attracted and entertained women. He was quite well off and had the kind of rugged and rangy masculinity that swarms of women hunted down. Unlike her, they'd be willing to overlook his gruffness.

She knew by the heat in her cheeks that her embarrassment was obvious, but she was also just as sure Max wouldn't miss an opportunity to make her suffer further for her foolishness.

'Now let me see.' He cocked his head to the ceiling as if considering her question. 'How is it that I know so much about women's breakfast habits?'

His eyes narrowed as if he was giving this matter his undivided attention. 'I think I probably picked up some pointers—like women's belief in the importance of orange juice—from all those television advertisements.'

Totally flustered and unable to think of an appropriate retort, Gemma concentrated very carefully on holding Mollie's cup at just the right angle for her to drink easily.

'But it beats me if I can remember just how I uncovered the mysterious feminine desire to dine first thing in the morning on low-fat yoghurt and muesli. That really has me stumped.' Relaxing back in a wooden kitchen chair, he joined his hands behind his head with elbows pointing to the ceiling. 'I guess I found out about European women's predilection for coffee and croissants from some foreign movie.'

'For heaven's sake,' Gemma growled at him. 'Good luck to any long-suffering woman who's had breakfast with you. The poor thing would need a ton of luck and a truckload of tolerance to put up with your chauvinism.'

He took a deep swig of iced water and chuckled. 'I'd say you're probably right.' Setting the glass back on the table, he grinned at her. 'You'll be able to find out to-morrow morning, won't you?'

'I think I could do without your early-morning charm,' she sniffed. 'And Mollie and I will have soft boiled eggs and toast soldiers for our breakfast.'

She turned away from his mocking grin and made a fuss of Mollie. But it was difficult to stop her mind from dwelling on the unexplored area of this conversation— the particular circumstances that led to a woman sharing breakfast with Max.

They didn't bear thinking about.

And yet, in spite of her efforts to ignore such offen-sive details, an unbidden picture planted itself firmly in Gemma's mind. A vision of a lamp-lit bedroom—with cool, white sheets—and Max's brown, muscle-packed back encircled by softly rounded, pale and feminine arms. A night of intimacy...

She felt an unpleasant wave of panic.

Would Max Jardine be charming in the company of other women?

Surely not.

'Do you have any bananas?' she asked, in a desperate bid to change the subject and to rid herself of these extremely unsettling thoughts. 'I—I could mash one for Mollie's lunch while you set up her cot.'

His eyes surveyed the kitchen. 'No bananas, I'm afraid. You might have to give her some of the tinned stuff we brought with us. I'll take a run into town first thing tomorrow morning. We should make up a shopping list.'

Gemma was so grateful they were no longer talking about Max's women that she spent the afternoon being particularly obliging and co-operative. Max made cold roast beef sandwiches for their lunch and they ate them at a table on the side verandah and washed them down with huge mugs of strong tea while Mollie played with her blocks on the floor nearby. Out in the paddocks the white cockatoos screeched raucous greetings as they returned to the grass seed to feed.

Then, after lunch, as Max had never bothered with a housekeeper, together they dusted and vacuumed spare rooms for her and Mollie's use. They set up Mollie's folding cot and her other equipment in a bedroom on the cool side of the house, with doors opening onto the verandah.

Gemma's bedroom was right next door. She had stayed in it before—a pretty room, very feminine, with pink and white curtains and a white candlewick bedspread on the old-fashioned iron bed. The bed-ends were decorated with shiny brass knobs and pretty pieces of porcelain painted with rosebuds.

She was startled to see a silver-framed photo of Dave and herself on the mahogany dressing table. It had been taken five years ago—in the days before Dave met Isobel—when Gemma was eighteen and she and Dave had still been 'going together'. Their liaison had been a casual arrangement that they'd drifted into as they grew older. She'd come back from university for his twenty-first birthday.

In the photo, they were dancing. Dave, dressed in a formal dinner suit, was laughing, and she was smiling at the camera and looking very pleased with herself in a pale blue evening gown with thin straps, a fitted bodice and a softly floating, long skirt. There were tiny white flowers dotted through her dark brown hair. At the time, she'd thought she looked very romantic.

Now she shuddered as a painful memory forced itself on her.

The night of Dave's party had ended with a shameful and embarrassing incident. A scene she had worked desperately hard to forget over the years. Surely Max had wanted to forget it, too? At the time he had been as upset as she was about what happened.

Shaking, she turned to him now. 'Why didn't you throw this old photo away?'

Max set down her suitcase, straightened and frowned in its direction. An unreadable emotion flashed in his eyes and his mouth tightened. After a moment, he said with a shrug, 'Didn't cross my mind.'

Rigid with tension, it took Gemma a moment or two to take in his words. Then relief flooded her. He must have forgotten what had happened that night! Either that or the incident that had caused her so much grief over the years had never really bothered him. Gemma forced herself to shrug as nonchalantly as he had. 'Fair enough,' she said.

She knew she should be relieved, but it took some time for her to feel calm again and to convince herself that she was happy with his detached reaction.

By evening, they had worked out how to barricade off the section of the verandah adjacent to the study, so that

Mollie could have a safe area to crawl and play while
Gemma worked. Gemma had unpacked her clothes and
had showered to wash off the dust from her journey.
She'd bathed the baby girl in the old claw-foot tub in
the main bathroom and fed her mashed vegetables. Max
had ambled down to one of the ringers' huts to discuss
station matters and explain about his visitors.

When he returned, he fixed a simple supper of steaks
and salad while Gemma gave Mollie her bottle and settled her for sleep.

Everything went like clockwork. Gemma couldn't believe how obliging Mollie was and how conciliatory
Max had been. She was beginning to feel calm and confident and even optimistic about the whole venture.
Surely this mood wouldn't last?

They ate together, and their steaks were followed by
a simple, no-frills dessert of chocolate chip ice cream
and tinned apricots. Then coffee. They chatted about
people they both knew from around the district and Max
was a surprisingly entertaining host—slipping humorous
anecdotes and juicy titbits of gossip into the conversation.

As he drained the last of his coffee, he put his cup
down and leaned back in his chair. 'I should have offered you a nightcap. Would you like a liqueur or
brandy?'

She shook her head. 'No, thank you. I'm quite tired,
but you have one.'

'Not tonight.' He looked at her thoughtfully. 'You
haven't told me anything about the trip you made to
England after university.'

'I didn't think you'd be interested,' she answered
stiffly.

His eyebrows rose the tiniest fraction. 'I don't need a

travelogue, but I'd like to know whether you found what you were looking for.'

The coffee cup in Gemma's hand rattled against its saucer. 'I went to London for two years' work experience.'

After a little, Max said, 'I suspected you were running away.'

He'd dropped the charm and reverted to Big Brother mode and Gemma's sense of relaxation was falling away at breakneck speed. She should have known the truce had been too good to last. 'What would I have been running away from?'

He frowned. 'You and Dave were so close for so many years. Everyone in the district thought of you as a couple.'

'Yes, but I'm sure everyone knew it wasn't serious.' She was stunned to think that Max might have thought she'd been pining after Dave. 'Heavens, Max, Dave and I just sort of hung out together out of habit. I mean— being with him was always fun and sweet and everything, but when we parted it was quite painless and definitely for the best.' She added quietly, 'There was something missing in our relationship.'

Heat leapt into her cheeks. She didn't add that there had seemed to be something missing in every relationship she'd attempted. Gemma had a dreadful suspicion that there was something missing in her own personality. She feared she just wasn't suited to romance. No matter how handsome and charming and eager to please her the young men she'd met had been, none of then had ever once made her feel giddily, genuinely in love. Not the kind of love she was hoping to find.

'You thought you would find that missing *some-*

thing…in London?' Max's eyes were lit with a puzzling intensity.

Blue fire.

The way their gaze locked onto hers robbed her breath. This man of all people shouldn't be asking her such questions.

'No, I wasn't hoping for that,' she said at last, and prayed that he couldn't guess she was lying through her teeth.

'No suave English gentleman swept you off your feet?'

It was time to finish this conversation. Gemma didn't like it at all. She especially didn't like the way her heart began beat so frantically when Max looked at her.

Unless she put an end to this now, she might end up admitting to him that although she'd met plenty of nice young men, none of them had captured her heart. And the very last thing Gemma wanted was for him to continue this line of questioning and uncover her embarrassing secret.

None of her family or friends knew the truth about her love life. Or rather her lack of a love life. Gemma was quite certain that she was the only twenty-three-year-old female outside a nunnery who was still a virgin.

She lifted her chin to what she hoped was a challenging angle. 'There were several men,' she told him. 'But, Max, you're not *my* big brother. I'm not giving you an itemised account and you don't need to keep watch over me. It's none of your business how many men I've met or—or how many affairs I've had.' Pushing back her chair, she jumped to her feet. 'I haven't asked you one tiny question about your breakfast companions.'

He stood also and looked down at her from his menacing height. 'What would you like to know?' he asked while a poorly suppressed grin tugged at the corners of his mouth.

'I have absolutely no interest in your philanderings.' She spun on her heel and began to stomp away from the table. Then she stopped abruptly, remembering her manners. 'I'll help you clear the table and tidy the kitchen,' she mumbled.

'Thank you, Gemma,' he replied with a studied politeness that annoyed her.

In silence they worked, Max gathering up the plates and cutlery, Gemma collecting the cups, place mats and serviettes. Together they walked into the kitchen and set their things down at the sink. They both reached for the tap at the same time. Their hands connected.

As if she'd been burnt, Gemma snatched her hand away from the contact, but Max's reaction was just as quick and he caught her fingers in his strong grasp.

His thumb stroked her skin once, twice...and she felt her blood stirring in response. Her hand trembled.

She wanted to pull away, but she was too fascinated by her body's astonishing reaction. Never had she felt so unsettled, so fired up by a man's simple touch. She didn't dare look at Max. She stood by the sink, mesmerised by the sight of her slim white hand in his large, suntanned grip. She could see little hairs on the back of his hand, bleached to gold by the sun. A faint trace of the fresh, lemon-scented soap he'd used in the shower still clung to his skin and his work-roughened thumb continued to move slowly over her hand, making her feel shivery and breathless.

'Gem.' His gruff voice barely reached her over the savage drumbeat in her ears.

She couldn't move, couldn't speak.

'Gemma,' he said again, and his other hand reached

under her chin, forcing her head up until their eyes met.
Max was looking as startled as she felt. His breathing
sounded just as hectic.

When his fingers began to trace ever so gently the
outline of her face, she could feel her skin flame at his
touch.

'Gemma Brown,' he whispered, 'whether you like it
or not, I'm going to keep watching you...just like I always have.'

And the moment was spoiled. Gemma was embar-
rassingly disappointed.

'For Pete's sake!' she exclaimed, wrenching her hand
out of his grasp and pulling right away from him. She
was fearfully angry with him and she wasn't quite sure
why. 'You are not my brother, my bodyguard or my
guardian angel!' For a dreadful moment she thought she
might burst into tears. 'Go paint some more walls. Get
a life, Max, and leave me to get on with mine!'

This time she didn't care about good manners.
Gemma rushed out of the kitchen and left him with the
dirty dishes.

CHAPTER THREE

THE grimy dishes were still sitting on the counter top waiting to be washed when Gemma walked into the kitchen the next morning. Added to last night's pile were an extra-greasy frying pan, a mug and more plates—things Max must have used for his breakfast before he headed off at sunrise.

'Who does he think he is?' she asked Mollie as she surveyed the dreary mess. Mollie merely whimpered and rubbed her face against Gemma's shoulder. She'd been restless during the night and still seemed rather fragile this morning. Having slept very fitfully, Gemma wasn't feeling too chipper either. In their own separate ways, both Max and Mollie Jardine had kept her tossing and turning for hours.

She set Mollie down on the floor while she hunted through Max's cupboards for a saucepan to boil their eggs, but Mollie began to cry almost as soon as Gemma walked away from her.

'Aren't you going to let me do anything this morning?' Gemma sighed. She tried to cheer the baby up with clucking noises while she set about making their breakfast.

After popping two eggs into a pot of water, she slid bread into the toaster and boiled the kettle for a mug of tea for herself. The phone rang. Gemma glanced at Mollie, who was still making miserable little whimpers and she deliberated whether she should let the answering machine deal with the call. Then, having second thoughts, she handed the baby a saucepan lid, hoping it would keep her happy while she dashed to the phone.

The call was from Brisbane—the printers were wanting to clarify some final details about the pamphlet—so Gemma was glad she'd answered. But when she returned to the kitchen, her heart sank.

Max stood in the middle of the room, with his hands on his hips, staring in dismay at Mollie, who was howling loudly and banging the saucepan lid on the floor in time to her wails.

She dashed into the room and swept the baby into her arms. 'Why didn't you pick her up?' she challenged Max, deciding to attack him before he could begin to accuse her of neglect.

But he clearly didn't react well to being scolded. His eyes narrowed. 'Where were you?' he asked.

'Where was *I*?' She knew she sounded shrewish, but was too frazzled to care. 'After pacing the floorboards all night, trying to calm your niece, I was answering an important business call. Where were *you*?'

'I've had one or two things to attend to,' he snapped. 'I need to talk to my men—delegate more jobs now that I have other responsibilities.'

'Who are you trying to kid?' Gemma cut in. 'You wouldn't recognise a responsibility if it was formally introduced to you. Who rocked Mollie back to sleep when she wouldn't settle last night? Me! Who waltzed off this morning without a care in the world and left the kitchen covered in grease? You did!'

'I'm sorry you had a bad night,' he replied with annoying composure, 'but calm down, Gemma.' He reached over and lifted the miserable Mollie from her arms. 'I had every intention of doing the dishes—same as I always do them—at lunchtime.'

'Lunchtime?'

Gemma might have launched into another tirade, but she noticed that Max's nose had begun to twitch. Was he feeling angry or just very guilty? Neither of the above, she realised with dismay as the acrid smell of smoke reached her.

'It seems you've burnt the toast,' he said quietly.

Black smoke billowed from the corner of the kitchen and Max, with Mollie on one hip, lunged across the room, switched the toaster off and flung its doors open.

Wasn't it just typical of this man? Gemma thought as she watched him. He could buy himself a smart little plane, a satellite dish and a fancy computer and still not have progressed to a pop-up toaster.

On the stove, the eggs were boiling so rapidly they rattled against the saucepan. 'Oh, blast! They'll be hard-boiled!' she wailed. This was definitely *not* her morning.

She snatched the saucepan from the stove, thumped it into the sink, then whirled around to glare at Max. He was nuzzling Mollie's tummy with his nose and making her laugh.

Laugh! Out loud!

Proper chuckles!

Gemma could feel her bottom lip drooping into a pout. How dared Mollie be so sweet and responsive to Max when she was the one who'd lost all the sleep? She sagged against the kitchen bench and, with a self-pitying sigh, folded her arms across her chest.

Max glanced at her. 'I'll take her out to see the puppies and give you some space to have another go at cooking breakfast,' he suggested.

She drew in a deep breath and nodded. Some peace and quiet, some space...that was what she needed...

And yet she felt strangely abandoned watching Max

take Mollie outside—as if they belonged together and she was the outsider. He carried her so easily, without any sense of awkwardness. He would make a good father... She found herself wondering how many of Max's breakfast companions had been hoping to marry him, to have him father their children.

Groaning at the stupid direction of her thoughts, Gemma picked up the blackened pieces of toast and, with grimly compressed lips, tossed them into the bin before setting out to remake breakfast.

By the time Max and Mollie returned, she had set the little table on the verandah and her breakfast and Mollie's were ready. She had decided against eggs after all and had made Mollie some porridge, settling for tea and toast for herself. And she'd assumed Max might want some more to eat so had made extra for him.

'Thanks,' he said as he settled Mollie on his lap and proceeded to feed her milky porridge with a tiny spoon.

'We could do with a high chair. It would make mealtimes much easier,' Gemma commented as Max intercepted Mollie's plump little hand before she could dunk it into the porridge bowl.

'I'll add it to my shopping list, but I'm not sure if Goodbye Creek runs to high chairs.'

'So you're going into town this morning?'

He nodded. 'Want to come?'

Gemma hesitated and took a sip of tea, shocked by her ready willingness to accept his offer. The idea of going to town with Max seemed more appealing than she could have thought possible. Her mind ran ahead of her, wondering what she might wear.

He was looking at her thoughtfully. 'Of course, you might appreciate some time to set up your office. I could take Mollie with me and get her out of your hair for the morning, while you get your business sorted out. It's a hot day for travelling and seeing you've had a rough night…'

Gemma placed her mug carefully back on the table. What on earth was wrong with her? Max Jardine was offering to get out of her way. She should be celebrating. This time yesterday she would have *paid* him to stay away.

His suggestion that she take the morning to reorganise her business was so brimming with common sense that she couldn't refuse without looking foolish. So why on earth did it make her feel downright miserable? Her tiredness had to be the answer—plus the fact that she had already grown so attached to Mollie that she hated to be parted from her.

'A morning to myself would be great,' she told Max brightly. 'You finish your toast and I'll go clean up Mollie and make up an extra bottle for you to take.'

'Better give me some extra clothes for her, too,' Max said as she stood to go. 'We might be some time.'

They were gone for most of the day. Many, many times Gemma went to the front verandah to peer down the dirt track, searching for the cloud of red dust on the horizon that would tell her the truck was returning. She hadn't the courage to tell Max that there wasn't much work on her books at present. He already had a low enough opinion of her without adding fuel to his fire.

But by ten o'clock in the morning she'd finished her work and she spent the rest of the day roaming restlessly around the house.

After lunch, she washed and dried all the dishes, vowing that she would have to change some of Max's bachelor habits. Then she set a sprinkler on the front lawn and picked some flowers from the old rambling garden that Max's grandmother had established many, many years ago. Exotic-smelling white gardenias, roses in two shades of pink and some yellow crucifix orchids.

After arranging the flowers in a crystal vase on the hall table, she piled a blue bowl with tangy bush lemons and set it on the kitchen dresser, then brought in Mollie's washing from the line, folded it and put it away.

By mid-afternoon, Gemma wondered if she should start thinking about the evening meal, but decided to wait and see what Max had bought.

At about four, a trail of dust signalled their return at last. Trying not to hurry, she made her way through the house to greet them, unable to disguise her pleasure when they pulled up near the kitchen door.

Max grinned at her as he swung his long frame down from the driver's seat and her heart gave a silly little lurch. He held a finger to his lips. 'Mollie's asleep,' he whispered. 'I'll try to get her out without disturbing her.'

Expertly, he unbuckled Mollie's car seat and lifted her gently out of the truck. In his strong arms, the baby girl looked comfortable and safe and Gemma's throat constricted painfully. The combined effect of Max's surprisingly tender manner as he handled his little niece and the way his usually grim gaze softened when he looked at her lying asleep in his arms upset her.

He hunched one broad shoulder forward to accommodate the little head covered in damp curls and the thoughtful gesture touched her deeply. But Gemma didn't want her emotions to be touched—such reactions were out of order and made her distinctly uncomfortable.

She felt better when she set about the businesslike task of unloading groceries and carting them through to the kitchen.

'How was town?' she asked when Max joined her.

'Same as always.' He shrugged. 'Mollie caused quite a stir.'

'I guess babies are a bit of a rarity out this way.'

He nodded and continued the unloading without further comment. He brought in a rather battered-looking high chair, which he proudly announced he'd found in the secondhand shop, and then he carried through an Esky full of cold goods and began to load the freezer with more tubs of chocolate chip ice cream and packets of frozen corn cobs and peas.

At last he looked up. 'Get plenty of work done while we were away?'

'Oh,' Gemma replied, with a vague wave of her hand, 'yes—heaps.'

'Mollie's been awake for most of the day. So many people wanted to make a fuss of her. I'd say she needs a good sleep now.'

'I guess so,' Gemma agreed. With a plastic scoop, she transferred sugar from a huge hessian bag into an old-fashioned metal canister. 'Would you like some afternoon tea?'

He glanced at his watch. 'I should mosey on down to the ringers' place and have something there. I need to know if Chad and Dingo were able to fix the pump on the five-mile bore.'

With that, he reached for the Akubra hat hanging on a nail near the back door and was gone.

Gemma clamped the lid down tight on the sugar canister, lugged the bag into the pantry, then sat down at the kitchen table and propped up her chin with her hand. She stayed there staring at the door where Max had disappeared. The clock on the wall ticked loudly.

Running her fingers through her short hair, she let out

a long sigh. A gloomy sense of depression settled on her, like a thick, suffocating fog.

Just why she felt so low was a puzzle.

She knew she should be delighted with how well this whole babysitting business was progressing. Instead of snarling at her and constantly annoying her, Max was keeping his criticisms to a minimum and, for the most part, he was being polite. If she overlooked the matter of the washing up, he was going out of his way to be co-operative. And instead of hanging around and making her nervous all day long, he was giving her space. He much preferred the company of his ringers to hers.

Was she imagining it, she wondered, or was he actually avoiding her?

Why should it matter?

The blast of a car horn sounded outside. A visitor. Gemma jumped to her feet and hurried down the hallway to find a dusty sedan pulling up at the front of the homestead. The driver's door swung open and a woman with a mass of bright red hair emerged. As Gemma watched, she opened the back of her car and, when she leaned in to retrieve something, the denim of her jeans stretched sinfully over well-rounded buttocks.

Gemma's eyebrows rose. Their visitor was wearing a sheer white blouse through which her lacy bra was clearly visible. It was tucked into the tightest jeans she'd ever seen.

'Yoo-hoo! Maxie!' the woman called as she straightened again. In one hand she was holding what looked like a casserole dish wrapped in a tea towel. She slammed her car door shut and began to sashay on very high heels towards the stairs.

Was this one of the breakfast ladies?

Gemma found herself studying the woman very carefully. Her age, she guessed, would be just the other side of thirty, and there was really only one word to describe her figure—curvaceous. On a highway, such curves would come with a sign warning danger. Except, Gemma noted grimly, these curves came in all the right places—exactly where men were supposed to want them.

Lucky Max.

When she saw Gemma standing on the verandah, the visitor paused.

'Hi,' Gemma called.

'Hello,' came the cautious reply. It was very clear to Gemma that the woman was shocked to see her there. She stood staring, her eyes popping and her carefully painted mouth wide open.

After an uncomfortable stretch of silence, Gemma asked, 'Are you looking for Max?'

'Yes… I am…' The visitor tossed her mane of gleaming red hair, like an animal preparing for a battle.

Gemma pointed to the dirt track leading away from the homestead and towards the ringers' huts. 'He's down there.'

'With Dingo?'

She nodded. 'I'm sure you're welcome to go on over, if you want to see him.' Coming down the steps, she held out her hand. 'Or perhaps I can help you?'

A petulant frown marred the woman's otherwise pretty features. 'I don't know,' she muttered. 'You see, I was expecting…' She fiddled with the tea towel that covered the container she was holding. Her fingernails were very long and painted to match her hair. 'I thought…' Then, with an embarrassed shrug, she shoved the covered dish towards Gemma. 'Here, you might as well take this. It's a casserole. I didn't know there was a woman here, though. You see, I thought Max was trying to look after the little baby on his own and I figured he might need a hand.'

Gemma offered the woman her sweetest smile. 'How kind of you, but I don't know if I should accept this meal. That's why I'm here. To help Max out. We're caring for Mollie together.'

'I wonder why Max didn't mention you.'

Gemma shrugged. She'd been wondering the same thing.

'You're not from round these parts, are you?'

'Not any more, but I grew up out here. I'm Gemma Brown. An old friend of…of the family and I'm the baby's godmother.' She extended her hand.

It was accepted reluctantly. 'Sharon Foster. I own Sharon's Hair Affair, the beauty salon in town. Max dropped by this morning.'

'Nice to meet you, Sharon. He just…dropped by…did he?'

'He was tickled pink to show off the kid.'

Gemma struggled to imagine Max in a beauty salon, surrounded by women all fussing over Mollie. 'Can I offer you a cup of tea or coffee, or a cold drink?'

Sharon shook her head and she gave Gemma the distinct impression that she'd choke on anything she gave her. 'No. I'll be right, thanks.'

'And you're sure you don't want to see Max ?'

There was a long moment of hesitation during which Gemma was subjected to a lengthy scrutiny. Eventually Sharon made up her mind. 'No. No, I won't bother him. Look, you might as well keep the casserole. There's only enough for two.'

'Thank you.'

'It's beef stroganoff.' Sharon looked smug. 'I know it's Max's favourite.'

'Really?' Gemma murmured with teeth clenched in a grimacing smile. 'You're so thoughtful. I'm sure he'll just gobble it up. What a pity you can't wait to see him after coming so far out of your way.' She knew the drive from town took at least an hour. Now this woman faced the long, dusty drive back.

'Yeah, well… Might see you some time,' Sharon said uncertainly and without the slightest effort at sincerity. She turned and tottered back to the car. Her departure was accompanied by a slamming of doors and a roaring acceleration down the track.

As Gemma walked back into the house, trying not to think about other times Max and Sharon Foster had shared beef stroganoff, she heard the unmistakable sounds of Mollie waking. She hurried to attend to her and had just finished changing her nappy when the phone rang. Balancing Mollie on her hip, she dashed to answer it.

'Hello, Goodbye Creek Station.'

'Er…hello,' replied a woman's voice. 'Do I have the right number? Is that the Jardines' place?'

'Yes.'

'*Max* Jardine's?'

'Yes, that's right. Were you wanting to speak to Max?'

'Oh…er, yes, please.'

'I'm sorry. He isn't in at the moment. Can I take a message.'

'Excuse me, but who is this?'

'Gemma Brown. I'm…a…I'm looking after Max's niece.'

'Oh! *Oh*…I see. I didn't realise he'd hired a nanny.' The feminine voice was mellow and sophisticated.

Gemma resisted the urge to let out a loud, exasperated sigh. 'He didn't actually hire me. I'm a close family friend—Mollie's godmother.'

'I see,' the caller said again, with less enthusiasm.

'Can I be of any help?'

'Uh…this is just a social call, really. I met little Mollie in town this morning. Max dropped past my surgery to say hello.'

'He took Mollie to a doctor's surgery?' Alarmed, Gemma took another look at the baby in her arms. She seemed healthy enough. 'Was there something wrong with her? Max didn't mention any problems.'

'Oh, no. It wasn't a professional visit. We're just…' The caller paused to indulge in a self-conscious little laugh. 'Max and I are just good friends. And he was so excited about his little niece, he just had to show her to me.'

'I'm sorry, I didn't catch your name.'

'I'm Helena Roberts-Jones, the local GP.'

The hairdresser, the doctor… With a nasty blaze of anger, Gemma wondered how many more of Max's women she would have to deal with.

'I'll tell Max you called,' she said in saccharine tones. 'It's good to know there's medical help nearby if we need it—especially with a baby in the house.'

'Thank you,' came the subdued reply. 'Goodbye, Gemma. Perhaps we'll meet up some time?'

'That would be nice.'

'Oh, one more thing,' Helena Roberts-Jones purred. 'Could you do me a tiny favour?'

'I—I guess so.'

'Could you please check with Max if he needs me to order him a dinner suit for the Mungulla Ball?'

'Sure. With pleasure,' muttered Gemma.

She dropped the receiver in its cradle and, with teeth clamped together, made her way to the kitchen, to find Mollie a drink. 'Who'll be next, Moll?' she asked the innocent baby in her arms. 'The local schoolmarm?' Luckily, Mollie wasn't perturbed by her godmother's tension. She simply chuckled and played with the gold chain at Gemma's neck.

With Sharon's casserole safely deposited in a slow oven, Gemma wandered through to the large and comfortable lounge room and settled on the softly carpeted floor to play with Mollie and try to forget about Max's harem. Not that she really cared how many of the local females he courted, she told herself.

But she did object to being thrust into the role of his social secretary.

Nevertheless, she was surprised and a little taken aback by the interest of these women. Yesterday, when the little issue of breakfast had arisen, Gemma had decided Max was teasing her. But now she wasn't quite so sure. In spite of the comments various women had made from time to time about his looks, she'd never really thought of him as a ladies' man. Surely he was too stern and aloof?

For the next half-hour, Gemma lolled on the lounge room carpet and built towers out of blocks for Mollie to knock over. And she played peek-a-boo using a huge velvet cushion. Each time she reappeared from behind the soft blue cushion, the baby squealed with delight.

'Someone's having fun,' came a deeply masculine voice.

Gemma lowered the cushion to find two dusty riding boots in front of her. She looked up.

'Boo,' grinned Max.

'Good evening,' she replied primly. She didn't enjoy finding herself kneeling at Max Jardine's feet. She struggled to stand.

'Don't let me spoil the fun,' he said. 'Stay there. I'm going to crack open a beer. Would you like a drink?'

About to snap back with a negative reply, Gemma thought better of it. Her nerves were feeling distinctly frazzled. 'Yes, I'll have a beer, too.'

'Right you are.'

When he returned with two long glasses of icy cold beer, she left the floor and sat on one of the chintz-covered armchairs. Max relaxed into a deep chair opposite her and stretched his long legs in front of him. Mollie crawled over to him and patted his leg happily. He lifted her with one hand onto his knee. She crowed with delight.

Gemma hunted for something to say. She wanted to let off steam about Max's callers, but decided this was an occasion when she should put into practice her intentions to stay calm and collected. If she made a fuss, Max might think she cared about his women for the wrong reasons. 'Is the bore fixed?' she asked.

'Yes. Chad and Dingo are handy blokes to have around.' He took a long, thirsty swig of beer. 'You can meet them tomorrow night. They always come up here on Friday nights. I cook a roast and we have a few beers. Nothing flash, of course. As you know, social life in the bush is fairly quiet.'

Gemma felt her plans to be calm and uncritical flying out of the window. *'Quiet?'* she repeated. 'You surprise me, Max. From what I can see, your social life seems rather lively.'

'It does?'

'I mean if we start with the Breakfast Club...'

Max straightened and almost dropped Mollie off his knee. 'I beg your pardon?'

'Your lady friends. Your *breakfast* companions.'

'Gemma, what the hell are you talking about?'

'How about I start with Sharon Foster? Helena Roberts-Jones?'

He stared at her, obviously taken aback. Then he set Mollie back on the floor and downed his beer in one long gulp. 'Have you been spying on me or something?'

She shot him a searing look. 'I don't need to go searching for your women, Max. I've been beating them off with a stick all afternoon.'

'The hell you have. What do you mean?'

'There have been phone calls, casseroles, visitors in see-through blouses and skin-tight jeans.'

He had the grace to frown and look confused as if she were talking in a foreign language. 'What on earth are you raving on about?'

'Ever since you came home from town there's been an endless stream of women callers.'

'Really?'

'Definitely. You and Mollie sure made a big impression this morning.'

'I must admit, I couldn't believe the way everyone carried on.'

'Well, you tried hard enough to get their attention... calling in at the beauty salon...dropping in on the lady doctor... I guess we'll hear from the school teacher next.'

At that very moment, the phone on the little side table rang.

'It'll be for you,' Gemma growled.

Max looked at the telephone as if it were a venomous snake about to bite him. Gingerly, he lifted the receiver.

'Jardine speaking.'

As he listened to his caller, a red flush flared in his cheeks. 'Susan? What a...surprise.' His hand fiddled with the collar of his shirt, as if it was too tight. 'A *nice* surprise, of course.' He turned, so that he was no longer facing Gemma. 'That's very thoughtful of you, Susan. *Tonight?* Well, actually, I think...'

Gemma picked up Mollie and, with a grim little smile, quietly left the room.

CHAPTER FOUR

FROM outside the lounge room, Gemma could still hear Max's low coaxing tones as he murmured into the phone. He seemed to be placating his caller's ruffled feathers. But, not wanting to eavesdrop on his conversation with Susan—the schoolmarm or librarian, or whoever she was—Gemma shut the elegant French doors which separated the lounge and dining areas.

She decided to do justice to Sharon Foster's meal by setting the table in the formal dining room, so she carried Mollie and her high chair through from the kitchen. In the linen cupboard, she found a delicate white lace tablecloth, which she spread over the polished timber table. As a centrepiece, Gemma set the vase of flowers she'd arranged earlier in the afternoon and two silver candlesticks holding slim, pale blue candles.

After a moment's hesitation, she approached the magnificent English oak sideboard and discovered a set of very good quality silverware and an exquisite blue and white Wedgwood dinner service.

'It's a pity to have all this going to waste,' she told Mollie.

She finished setting the table, lit the candles and stepped back to observe her work with a critical eye. The overall effect was surprisingly pretty.

By the time Max sauntered through the French doors, Mollie was halfway through her meal. He and Susan had had a jolly long phone call, Gemma thought grumpily.

'You'll be happy to know that Susan isn't a school

teacher,' he announced, before nonchalantly shoving his hands in the pockets of his jeans and rocking back on his heels. 'She's the post mistress.'

Blast him! It was only because she knew the quality of the tableware that Gemma resisted the temptation to bang something. She squared her shoulders and eyed him with as much haughty disdain as she could muster. 'I don't care if the entire Australian women's basketball team are interested in you. They can phone you—or drop by—as often as they like. Just as long as I don't have to keep taking their calls.'

'I'm sorry you've had to deal with this.' His attention was caught by the dimmed lights and the table. He eyed the candles with deep suspicion. 'Are we—am *I* expecting company?'

Gemma suppressed a smile. 'No, but we have something special for dinner, so I thought I should make an effort. Can you finish feeding Mollie while I fetch our food?'

'Sure.'

As she moved away, Max called after her. 'You might be interested to know that I put a call through to the embassy in Somalia as well. I managed to speak to Isobel.'

Poor Isobel! Guiltily, Gemma turned back. 'That's wonderful. How is she? Has she seen Dave?' How could she have become so caught up in her own grumbles about Max that, for a moment, she'd almost forgotten about her friends' horrendous situation?

'Actually, she sounded very tired and depressed. She's only just arrived in Somalia, so she hasn't been able to see Dave yet. There's a certain amount of red tape to get through first.' His mouth twisted into a half-hearted smile. 'I did my best to cheer her up.'

Gemma stepped towards him and rested her hand on his arm. He was standing with a spoonful of Mollie's dinner in one hand and her bowl in the other. At Gemma's touch, he froze. 'I'm sure she loved hearing from you. Don't worry about Dave,' she said gently. 'I have every faith that he will be OK.'

'Yeah, of course.' He nodded before continuing to spoon food into Mollie's waiting mouth with the precision of an expert.

'How did Isobel take the news about our decision to share minding Mollie?'

'Her initial reaction was stunned disbelief.'

'I'll bet it was. She knows I—I—well, she knows you and I aren't soul mates.'

Max grunted. 'Once she got over the first shock, she seemed to warm to the idea. And the Embassy have given Isobel an e-mail address, so we'll be able to keep her posted about how Mollie's doing and she'll keep us up to date as well.'

'That's great.'

When she returned from the kitchen with two plates of Sharon's beef stroganoff and a rusk for Mollie to chew on, Max sniffed appreciatively. 'Smells good.'

'You should enjoy this. It's a very special treat.'

'It is?'

She smiled sweetly. 'You don't recognise this tasty dish?'

Lifting a tentative forkful of the beef and mushroom mixture, he tasted it, chewed carefully and swallowed. He looked puzzled. 'I'm not totally familiar with the flavour. It's rather fancier than my usual meals.'

'Oh? Surely Sharon's not mistaken? She assured me this was your favourite.'

Max seemed to choke a little and reached for his water glass. 'My favourite?'

'Yes,' Gemma replied with a devilish sense of satisfaction. 'Sharon Foster cooked this for us with her own two hands—well, if I'm honest, it wasn't meant for *us* exactly—I'm sure she didn't plan for me to be enjoying her culinary efforts.'

He chewed thoughtfully. 'She's a good cook, isn't she? This is very tasty.'

Gemma wasn't going to give him satisfaction by admitting anything of the sort. 'After poor Sharon drove all the way out here this afternoon, I thought the least I could do was go to the trouble of setting the table nicely with candles and flowers. I've tried to reproduce the evening just how she would have wanted it for you.'

'Gemma,' Max asked, not trying to hide the glitter of scepticism in his eyes, 'are you being catty?'

Her cheeks grew uncomfortably warm. Trust Max to try to turn this situation against her. She took another mouthful of beef to give herself time to think of an answer.

He watched her obvious discomfort. 'I think I detect a little of the green-eyed monster.'

'Why on earth would I be jealous?' she exploded. 'That's utter nonsense, Max.'

'I'm relieved to hear it.'

Her hands clenched tightly in her lap. *Damn him!* How on earth could Max even begin to think that she was jealous of his women? Why, she was downright sorry for them. Wasting their feelings on a grumpy recluse like him. If the poor deluded souls were hoping to trap him into marriage, they had Gemma's heartfelt sympathy.

She glared at him. 'Isn't it enough that you have

Sharon, Helena *and* Susan all panting after you? Surely you don't expect me to go weak-kneed as well?'

He frowned and Gemma was forced to lower her own eyes, so that she didn't have to meet his piercing gaze. To her intense dismay, when he looked at her like that, she felt goose bumps forming on her arms. Surely he wasn't remembering that long ago time? A time that she'd rather forget.

His voice cut into her thoughts. 'So I'm safe from your affection. That's a weight off my mind.'

She wasn't looking at him, but she could tell by the sudden wariness in his tone that he was as uncomfortable talking about such matters as she was.

'You're very safe, Max. As far as I'm concerned, you've about as much sex appeal as toenail clippings!' She refused to look up.

'Oh, well,' he said with an exaggerated sigh. 'I guess three women out of four is not a bad score for a bloke from the bush.' Suddenly, the tension left his voice. 'Seriously, Gemma, it's not really all that surprising that Mollie's stirred up all this feminine interest.'

Her head shot up again. 'Only you could blame a stampede of women to your door on a helpless baby.' She glanced at Mollie innocently chewing on her rusk and rubbing moist crumbs all over her chubby, little face. 'You should be ashamed of yourself,' she cried. 'This *feminine interest* has nothing to do with Mollie.'

He smiled slowly. 'I must admit I didn't think about any repercussions when I headed for town. I just wanted to show off Dave's little daughter, but I should have gone to Helena first. She would have been able to warn me.'

'*Warn you?*'

'About the effects of a bachelor and a baby on women.

Apparently most women find it a pretty heady combination.'

'Oh?'

'Yeah. Didn't you know? A fellow with a baby is a real chick magnet.'

'*Chick* magnet?'

'That's what Helena told me.'

'That doesn't sound like the scientific terminology you'd expect from a doctor.'

'I wasn't visiting Helena for medical advice. She and I—'

'I know, I know,' Gemma cut in coldly. 'You're just good friends.'

'That's exactly right.' He shrugged and held out his hands, palms up, as if pleading innocence. 'Anyway, it seems that lots of females happen to find a single bloke with a baby kind of…irresistible, although you've remained quite untouched.'

Her chair scraped loudly against the polished timber floor as she jumped to her feet. 'That's because I've been overexposed to the single bloke in question. I'm sure the dear doctor would classify me as a hardened case.'

She made a fuss of wiping Mollie's face and forced a hard edge of sarcasm into her voice. 'It's just as well some of us are immune to your fatal charms, Mr Jardine. Half the women in the district have started behaving foolishly—throwing themselves all over you.' For a shocking moment she hesitated as an unwanted memory taunted her again. Her eyes caught his and she blushed before hurrying on. 'We—we can't let the entire Australian outback come to a grinding halt.'

Lifting Mollie out of the high chair, she dropped a light kiss on her head. 'I'm going to fix this little girl's bottle.'

At the dining room doorway she turned to face Max, still sitting at the table, a bemused expression on his face. 'By the way, I mustn't forget to give you a message from your *very* good friend, Dr Roberts-Jones. She must have been so busy imparting all that helpful information, she forgot to ask you if you need to hire a formal dinner suit for the Mungulla Ball. You are to let her know if you want one.'

She dashed away without waiting to hear his answer.

The next day, Gemma was spared an overdose of Max's company. He was busy with station matters all morning and he charged in at lunchtime with instructions for roasting the large piece of beef he'd extracted from the cold room the night before.

'The ringers will start dropping by around sunset, but they won't expect to eat straight away. Make sure there are plenty of potatoes,' he called as he raced off, leaving the fly-screen door to bang behind him and without so much as a passing glance at the pile of dirty dishes in the sink.

Scant minutes later, he dashed back and popped his head through the door again. 'Oh, and there's a Pommy Jackaroo joining us tonight. He's been working on Mungulla, but he's shown a flair for horse work, so I'm using him here for a few weeks.' His eyes darted to the sink and he hesitated, then sent her the grin of naughty schoolboy, who hadn't done his homework. 'Mind if I skip sink duty just this once?'

When he looked at her like that, Gemma felt a weird little pain in her chest. 'I hope you have a very good excuse.'

'This Pom and I are pretty busy trying to break in some extra horses. We're going to need more mounts this season because after the rain there's so much feed on the ground. It'll be dangerous using motorbikes for cattle work.'

Giving an exaggerated sigh, she held out her hands. 'If I get dishpan hands, you can pay for my next manicure.'

He touched one of her hands with his rough fingers and winked. 'If I speak to her extra nicely, Sharon might give you a slap-up manicure for free.' Then he dashed away again before she could reply.

At a quarter to six, shortly before sunset, Gemma heard Max's footsteps re-enter the house and head for the bathroom. She checked the oven. Assuming that the men would want to sit and enjoy a few beers before they ate, everything was coming along nicely. She'd added carrots, pumpkin and onions as well as the mandatory potatoes to the baking tray and she'd unearthed a deep-dish apple pie from the depths of the freezer.

For the occasion, she'd set the dining table again with the good china and silver and she'd dressed Mollie in a pretty little pink and white dress. Gemma had thought about dressing up, but understood enough about outback ways to know that this evening would be a casual affair. Nevertheless, she'd exchanged her usual cotton sundress for a pair of tailored white jeans and a sleeveless red silk shirt.

She was rather looking forward to the evening ahead. In the past she had enjoyed similar times, when she'd sat on the verandah, watching the sun go down and the stars come out, and listened to background drone of cicadas while the men swapped jokes and yarns about the bush. The men in the outback were always great storytellers. If the jokes became a bit rough, they would apologise to her, but they never made her feel unwelcome.

'The roast smells great.' Max came into the kitchen, with his hair wet from the shower and slicked back. He was still buttoning his light-blue cotton shirt and hadn't yet tucked it into his jeans. He smelled clean and spicy—the kind of smell that made Gemma's feeble brain think about getting closer.

Horrified by her reaction, she turned and took several steps clear away from him.

'Hey,' he said, watching her walk, 'you look…you… look… Do you think you should be wearing jeans like that when there'll be so many fellows around?'

'What's wrong with my jeans?'

'Well there's nothing *wrong* with them, exactly. That's the problem. They're just right. They look terrific. But you'll give these blokes ideas.'

'What kind of ideas?' she asked, pretending innocence.

'They might think you're—available.'

Feeling emboldened by his apparent discomfort, Gemma folded her arms and cocked her head to one side as she eyed him steadily. 'I had no idea I was *un*available.'

Max scratched his exposed chest and looked at her with a puzzled frown.

'What have you told them about me?' she persisted.

'Nothing. Absolutely nothing. Well—' He fiddled with one of his shirt buttons and Gemma wished he would hurry and get the shirt done up. She didn't need to see that broad, brown chest and those sleek, sculpted muscles. He cleared his throat. 'I've told them—just in case they got the wrong idea, you see—I've explained that you and I are not an item.'

'I—I'm very glad they understand that,' she muttered

while she hunted noisily through the saucepan cupboard to find a pot for boiling beans.

'But, unfortunately, they didn't really believe me.'

She found a suitable pot and thumped it down on the counter top. 'Well, what would they expect, Max? You have so many women who *are*—items. I suppose they've seen me about the place and leapt to a very logical conclusion.'

'Gemma, I think you might have been getting the wrong idea about me. I'm no lady-killer.'

Slowly and deliberately, he tucked the shirt tails into his jeans and Gemma swung her glance to the floor. It unnerved her to see him doing intimate things like that. The movements emphasised his manliness—the pleasing angle his body made as it tapered from his shoulders through to his hips—and it made her forget his problem personality. If she didn't rein in her thoughts right now, she might be lining up with Susan, Sharon and Helena.

'I never suspected that you *killed* ladies, ' she hissed, waving the saucepan at him.

'You're deliberately misunderstanding me.'

'I'm deliberately telling you to get out of here. Go play host while I—'

'While you play Cinderella? No way.' He stepped closer and grabbed her hand as it gripped the saucepan handle. 'We're partners, remember? I don't want you stuck in the kitchen like a meek little servant.'

If she were honest, it wasn't a role she fancied, either.

'Let's take Mollie and go out on the verandah and relax with a well-earned drink.'

When she followed Max outside, Gemma was relieved to find that the ringers, Chad and Dingo and a young apprentice they called Squirt, were just arriving. They all had a distinctly scrubbed-up look about them and reeked of after-shave, and they looked a little shy and awkward while Max made the introductions and handed round beer stubbies in polystyrene holders.

Gemma was contemplating breaking the ice with a question about their day, when another man appeared around the corner of the homestead and made his way onto the verandah. She knew at once that he must be the Pommy Jackaroo.

As he approached, his body silhouetted against the setting sun, he seemed to her to be every inch an Englishman. She watched him come closer and she could see that his skin had been burnt a ruddy brown in the outback, but his neat, light-brown hair, grey-blue eyes and dignified bearing marked him as coming from the same mould as many of the nicer young men she had met in London.

Max introduced the newcomer to Gemma as Simon Fox and he watched warily as the young man returned her greeting. Gemma couldn't help noting the way Max's eyes darkened while Simon's lit with appreciation as they exchanged a firm handshake. She was impressed when the young Englishman took the trouble to show polite attention to Mollie, who was sitting on Gemma's lap, blissfully sucking her toes.

Once Simon had accepted a beer and lowered his length into a low-slung squatter's chair, the conversation soon settled into a leisurely discussion of the importance of a good stock horse. Gemma listened with interest to the men's thoughts about the comparable benefits of motorbikes over horses for station work.

'There are plenty of places where a good stock horse will beat a motorbike hands down any day,' affirmed Dingo. 'For starters, there are far too many hills and gullies to the north of here for a motorbike and you'll always need a good horse for mustering and yard work.'

For a moment Gemma stopped listening as she thought about her own experiences in the bush and the excitement of a good muster. The smell of dust and the thrill of thundering hooves as her horse tore over the red soil plains. The heart-stopping danger as she watched the men catch and throw bullocks. And then there was the intense satisfaction of being part of a fast-paced, energetic team during yard work, when they branded, eartagged and vaccinated each beast inside a minute.

All through her high school years, when the wet season finished and the mustering began, Gemma had never missed the chance to join the team on Goodbye Creek station.

'You can't beat a horse for walking cattle and holding them,' she heard Chad drawl, before taking a deep thirsty swig at his beer.

She turned to Simon. 'And I understand you're something of an expert with horses?'

'I seem to have a bit of a knack,' he agreed modestly.

They exchanged friendly smiles.

'He's not too bad for a Pommy Jackaroo,' chipped in Dingo with a sly grin.

'Have you been in Australia very long?'

'Eighteen months. And that's too long, as far as my family are concerned,' he explained with a laugh.

'I guess they're missing you.'

'My father thinks I've done enough adventuring around the antipodes and it's time to come home and be of some use to the family.'

'They're farmers?' Gemma asked with genuine interest. Out of the corner of her eye, she sensed Max shifting restlessly on his chair.

'How's that roast?' he asked suddenly. ' You'll need to get the beans on by now, won't you?'

Lord, the man was a spoilsport! Gemma felt her anger flaring. For the first time since she'd arrived at Goodbye Creek someone was treating her like a human being and she was having a normal conversation that had nothing to do with babies, hormones or other people's love lives. She was tempted to tell Max to check his own roast, like he did every other Friday night when she wasn't there, but the men were all looking at her with an expectant air.

If she gave their boss a piece of her mind, she knew they would either be shocked to the soles of their riding boots, or they would assume she and Max had an 'understanding'—and that, married or not, she was his 'missus'.

That was the last thing she wanted them to think, so she rose and meekly handed Mollie over while she went to the kitchen to check the meal.

The roast was fine, the beans boiled beautifully and the rest of the evening went without a hitch. And after they had eaten and were replete with good food and fine wine, everyone moved back to the verandah. Gemma felt completely relaxed for the first time since she'd arrived at Goodbye Creek. Jokes and yarns were swapped, accompanied by the occasional slapping at a mosquito or the clink of glasses as they downed a nightcap.

After the men eventually left, she checked on Mollie and came back into the kitchen to find Max up to his elbows in hot sudsy water, tackling the washing-up straight away, rather than leaving it till the next day. Surprised, she took up a tea towel and quietly worked beside him.

She found it safer to look at the view through the

window over the sink than to watch his strong hands gleaming with soapy water, or his muscular arms with shirt sleeves rolled back. Outside, the moon was hanging high in the sky like a shiny saucepan lid. Bathed in its light, the paddocks looked pale and silvery. From down near the creek, she could hear a lone curlew calling.

She found herself thinking again about how much she loved the bush and how, at one time, ages ago, she had never expected to leave it. Now, the bush still felt like home—as if she belonged. And yet, any day soon, she hoped to hear from Isobel that Dave was safe and then they would be coming back for Mollie. Handing Mollie back to her mother meant returning to Brisbane.

Leaving the bush.

And Max.

'How long are you going to spend drying that one plate?'

His voice penetrated her cloud of thoughts and Gemma realised she'd been standing in a daze for ages and there was no more room on the dish rack. Hastily, she dumped the plate she'd polished bone dry and grabbed another.

Max shook his head in mock exasperation then picked up the baking dish and scratched at a blackened patch with the steel wool pad. 'Thanks for tonight,' he said. 'It's nice for a change to have the little feminine touches that I kind of gloss over, like flowers on the table, red wine, gravy…and apple pie.'

She smiled at him, and thought how different he looked when he wasn't frowning at her. She was beginning to understand why some women were attracted to Max. Well, lots of women, she had to admit. There were odd moments when he let his charm shine through—even for her.

And those charming moments had been getting to her recently, so that she'd found herself thinking about them when he was away during the day. She'd even thought about what it would be like when he really turned on the charm. The effect would probably be quite stunning.

Heart-stopping.

She wondered why he hadn't married. There didn't seem to be a shortage of volunteers for the job. Now that Dave was carving a different career path for himself, Max could do with someone to help him run the household as well as the property. When she thought about the amount of renovating he'd done in recent years, she realised that he'd been working extremely hard.

Surely it was a too much for one man to manage on his own?

She stood side by side with him, drying several more plates, and realised that a week ago she would never have dreamed of connecting Max and marriage.

'You and the Pommy Jackaroo seemed to hit it off,' he said, after they'd worked together some time. His blue eyes met hers, glanced away and met again, before he went back to scrubbing fiercely at the bottom of the blackened baking dish.

'Yes. He's a nice young fellow, isn't he?'

'"A nice young fellow,"' Max scoffed. 'You sound like somebody's grandmother.' He shot her a sceptical grimace. 'You two seemed to be cooking up something when he was in the kitchen helping you with dessert.'

She should have known that her eagle-eyed overseer wouldn't miss a trick. 'Actually,' she said quickly, deciding not to beat around the bush, 'Simon has asked me to go with him to the Mungulla Ball.'

Max's scrubbing movements stilled. 'The sneaky devil.' He let the baking dish slide beneath the suds as he rose to his full height and stared down at her. 'And you explained why you couldn't oblige, didn't you?'

Gemma lifted her chin. 'I certainly did not.'

'You didn't?' He let out a mirthless huff. 'For heaven's sake, Gemma, you'll have to explain to him first thing tomorrow that you can't go.'

'No way!' she cried defensively. ' I really want to go to that ball. It's for Ruth and Tom Neville's tenth wedding anniversary. You're going with Helena, aren't you?'

'She spoke to me about it weeks ago. I accepted before—before I knew about Dave—otherwise I would have—'

For several heartbeats, Gemma waited for him to finish the sentence, but it seemed he'd changed his mind. He was concentrating on rinsing the baking dish with fresh, hot water.

After the silence went on too long, she answered back. 'Well, Simon couldn't speak to me about it weeks ago. We only met tonight.'

'Exactly. That's my point. You hardly know the man.'

Gemma shook her damp tea towel at him. 'Max, can I remind once again that you are not *my* big brother? You don't have to worry about me. I really don't need you to vet my dates.'

'What about your other responsibilities? What about Mollie?'

'For Pete's sake!' For the second time tonight she felt like Cinderella. This time she was fighting for her right to go to the ball. 'Don't try to use Mollie as an excuse, Max. You know as well as I do that babies and children go to balls out here. You, Dave and I cut our teeth on outback balls. The Nevilles will have plenty of rooms set aside for the little ones to sleep in.'

Max eased his weight back against the sink with his hands folded across his chest and eyed her thoughtfully.

'I'm going, Max,' she challenged, stepping forward and jabbing a finger into his hard chest. 'And, what's more, I'm going to have the time of my life.'

He clasped her fingers in a hand that was warm and damp from washing up.

Something drastic happened to Gemma's ability to breathe. Max was holding her hand against his chest and, Lord help her, she was thinking how interesting it would be if he kept on hauling her closer.

His eyes were so very blue when they were this close. 'You've always been a mouthy little shrimp,' he said while his thumb massaged her fingers, her hand, her wrist. 'Have you any idea how you look when you're all fired up like that?'

His question hung in the silent room.

'No,' she whispered breathlessly.

Had she risen on tiptoes? Or was Max leaning closer? They seemed to be almost touching. What an incredible mouth he had. So sexy. 'How do I look, Max?'

'Definitely kissable,' he said in a voice that sounded half trapped in his throat.

Heaven help her! It was what she wanted him to say and what he mustn't say. His lips were on her forehead. She could feel them caressing her with their soft, warm pressure. His arms were coming round her and they felt sensational and she knew that any minute now his lips would seek hers.

But—but this was all wrong!

This was *Max!*

She knew that she couldn't let him kiss her!

Just in time, she struggled out of his embrace and

staggered backwards across the kitchen, her breathing ragged, painful, panting.

Max stood, still as a rock, with his back to the sink and his arms hanging empty at his sides. He regarded her with a steady, unsmiling gaze.

'You mustn't kiss me, Max.'

'No?'

Desperately, she shook her head.

'You're saving yourself for the Pommy Jackaroo?'

She didn't know what else to say, couldn't think how else to answer. 'I guess I am.'

At that, his face hardened into a blank mask. 'Then I wish you good luck.' He nodded curtly. 'And goodnight, Gemma.'

'Goodnight,' she echoed as he strode slowly out of the room.

Her shoulders sagged as she sank onto a kitchen chair. So close. She'd almost let Max kiss her.

But Gemma knew for certain that to kiss Max Jardine was to book a passage on the *Titanic*. She must make sure that he never tried to kiss her again.

CHAPTER FIVE

'I'M AFRAID I don't stock much formal wear.' Jessie Block, the stout and rather worried-looking owner of Goodbye Creek's one and only dress shop, shook her head gloomily. 'And I've almost nothing in your size, Gemma.'

With eyes the colour of faded denim, she studied Gemma and frowned.

'I'm too small?'

'Too small and too young,' sighed Jessie. 'All the young people get their clothes when they go to the city, or they have them sent out.'

'I haven't time to have anything sent out.'

It was already Wednesday, just a few days before the ball, but it was the first day Max had been free to babysit so that Gemma could escape into town to find something to wear. She'd known that at this late stage the chances of finding something suitable in a tiny outpost like Goodbye Creek were almost nil. She stared at the racks of Jessie's frocks and suppressed a grimace. They were mostly florals and prints in fabrics, styles and sizes suitable for the most conservative and matronly of souls.

She would just have to stick to the basic black that she'd thrown into her bag at the last minute. It had served her faithfully many times in the past and, while it was no longer the height of fashion and it definitely wasn't a ball gown, it would do at a pinch.

Jessie was rummaging around, shuffling coat hangers and desperately pulling out the most unlikely offerings.

'I'm sorry,' she said, as Gemma shook her head at a lime-green and feathered concoction. 'I really don't think I'm going to be able to help you.'

'That's OK,' Gemma reassured her. 'It was a stab in the dark thinking I might find something at this late stage.'

'What a pity.'

'Thanks for going to so much trouble.' Gemma slipped the strap of her bag back over her shoulder and turned to leave the shop.

'Wait a minute!' Jessie exclaimed. 'I've just remembered something. It's right at the back because it's never been suitable—' She darted excitedly to a rack at the back of the shop and hunted through a row of tired and outdated-looking clothes covered with plastic film. 'I'm sure it's still here,' she muttered.

But Gemma had resigned herself to wearing her black and she had no faith whatever in anything Jessie might unearth. 'Please, don't go to any more bother.'

'It's no bother,' came the predictable reply.

Gemma hovered near the doorway. Already she was thinking about what else she wanted to buy while she was in town. More formula for Mollie, a new toothbrush, some fresh oranges...

'Eureka!' shrieked Jessie. She charged back to Gemma, reverently holding a dusty plastic bag in front of her as if she were offering the Holy Grail. 'I'm sure it's your size,' she beamed.

As Jessie peeled away the plastic cover, Gemma eyed the garment dubiously. There seemed to be nothing of it. It looked more like a bundle of spangled cobwebs than a dress.

'It looks much better on,' urged Jessie.

It would need to.

'You'll try it?'

'Is it my size?'

Jessie nodded enthusiastically and led the way to the curtained cubicle at the back of the shop. 'Sing out if you need a hand,' she called as she drew the curtain closed.

Gemma was no longer in the mood for trying on clothes. Her eagerness had faded soon after she saw what was available. She was sure this dress would be no more suitable than the others. But, to please Jessie, she wriggled out of the trouser suit she'd worn into town and reached for the coat hanger.

The dress was so soft and shapeless Gemma took a few minutes to work out the front from the back and how exactly to put it on. Eventually, she slipped the cobweb-fine garment over her head. One arm slid into a slim, fitted sleeve while the other stayed bare as the dress slid over her breasts, past her waist and hips to skim her ankles. She took a deep breath and looked in the mirror.

And took another, sharper breath—more like a gasp.

'How are you going, dear?' Jessie called through the curtain.

'I'm almost ready,' Gemma replied. She needed a moment to examine the dress without Jessie fussing around her. She had to get used to the idea that this garment suited her. Suited her? It was amazing. When Cinderella's fairy godmother had waved her wand, she couldn't have achieved a more magical transformation.

The off-one-shoulder gown was soft and clinging and fitted her perfectly. Silvery blue, it looked as if it had been spun out of moonshine—and the sparkle it put into Gemma's light-blue eyes was quite amazing. She reached up and fluffed her short dark hair and, as she moved, she noticed long slits up each side of the skirt. 'Good, it will be suitable for dancing,' she said softly.

'What's that, dear?'

Time to put Jessie out of her misery. Drawing back the curtain, Gemma did an excited little spin. She was feeling great! 'What do you think?'

'Oh, my dear! Oh, Gemma! I knew it would be perfect!' Jessie circled around her, sighing with delight. 'You'll blow Max away with this!'

'Do you think so?'

'Oh, yes, love.'

Something nasty, like an electric shock zapped through Gemma. She clapped her hand to her mouth and wished with everything she had that she could take back this silly conversation. 'It's not what Max thinks that counts,' she hastily corrected. 'I'm not going to the ball with Max.'

Her words echoed over and over in her head. *I'm not going to the ball with Max.* And her sense of happiness and excitement drifted away, heading straight for the ground like dying autumn leaves.

Gemma covered her face with her hands and gave a little shake. This was so silly. She'd known all along she wasn't going with Max. So why had she been thinking about him when she first saw her reflection in the mirror?

'I'm going to the ball with Simon Fox,' she explained, looking Jessie squarely in the eye.

'Oh?' Jessie looked puzzled. 'Is he from around these parts, dear?'

'Yes.' Gemma laughed. 'Surely you've heard about the Pommy Jackaroo?'

'Oh, yes. Of course.' Jessie looked exceedingly embarrassed. 'I'm sorry. I just thought with you staying out at the Jardines' place to look after the baby and all—'

'Max is taking Dr Roberts-Jones.'

'Oh, I see.'

Gemma was startled by how forlorn Jessie looked. 'But I'm still going to buy this dress, Jessie. How much is it?'

The shopkeeper named a ridiculously cheap price. 'It's old stock,' she explained. 'And I'll never be able to sell it to anyone else.'

Once Gemma was back into her street clothes and the dress was paid for and carefully wrapped in lavender tissue paper, she found it easier to shrug off her sense of depression. Lately, she'd been letting herself get tied up in knots about Max. At night, she kept dreaming about him and the way he'd told her she looked kissable. What she had to remind herself, in the broad, bright light of day, was that Max had a string of women he told things like that.

And he would be taking one of them to the ball.

Besides, she might as well be positive. There was a very good chance that Simon Fox would find her kissable, too, and that was preferable any day to being kissed by Max Jardine.

But although Gemma gave an outward appearance of calm over the next few days, by the time Saturday, the day of the ball, arrived, she was as keyed up as a teenager on her first date.

Simon, Max, Mollie and Gemma had arranged to travel together to Mungulla and meet Helena there. All their party clothes were packed carefully into one suit pack, while in the back of the four-wheel drive they loaded tents and swags for sleeping plus Mollie's folding cot.

Gemma knew from past experience that many revellers would stay up and party all night, progressing

straight from dancing and drinking to the recovery
breakfast in the morning. But she was most definitely
planning to pitch a tent down by the creek and catch a
few hours' rest before breakfast and the long, dusty drive
home the next day.

On the journey, Gemma stayed in the back of the
cabin with Mollie, while the men sat in front, but she
was determined not to be left out of the conversation.
She wanted to get to know her partner better before she
found herself dancing in his arms all evening, and besides, there was so much to discuss about London.

Simon knew most of the pubs and restaurants she had
frequented while she lived there and they had also seen
many of the same shows. Their discussion warmed up
as they threw around names like Notting Hill Gate and
Richmond Park and Simon grew quite animated. As they
chatted, Max sat in grim, jaw-clenched silence, gripping
the steering wheel with whitened knuckles.

His moodiness reminded Gemma of the Max of old,
the Max who'd looked down on her girlhood friendship
with Dave, and it made her more determined than ever
to find Simon utterly fascinating.

They turned off the bitumen highway and rattled over
the gravel road that led into Mungulla station, past pale,
grassy paddocks dotted with skinny gum trees and sleek,
grey-coated Brahman cattle.

Simon turned back to Gemma. 'What a pity we didn't
cross paths while you were in London. I could have
taken you down to our farm in Devon.'

'Devon!' she exclaimed. 'I *loved* Devon. It would be
wonderful to—'

Crunch! At that moment, the vehicle swerved and hit
an enormous pothole. Gemma was thrown against the
door. Mollie woke up and began to cry and Simon, who

had only just managed to hold himself upright, turned smartly to the front again.

Gemma glanced suspiciously at Max's stiff back and her eyes caught his narrowed gaze in the rear vision mirror. She had the distinct impression that he'd hit that pothole in a deliberate attempt to stop their conversation. But if he thought he could prevent her from spending an enjoyable evening with Simon, he was going to be disappointed.

The sun was slipping low towards the distant rim of blue hills by the time they reached Mungulla. Many people had arrived ahead of them and their vehicles were parked in the shade of the huge paperbarks lining the crest of the bank that ran down to the creek. Trestle tables and chairs were set out on the stretch of lawn in front of the long, low homestead and in one corner a timber floor had been constructed for dancing. The African Tulip trees that framed the lawn were strung with lights.

'This is going to look absolutely gorgeous once it's properly dark,' Gemma said as she took in all the preparations.

They climbed out of the car and stretched their cramped legs.

Simon touched Gemma's arm and asked in his usual gentlemanly manner, 'Can I help you with Mollie's things?'

'She'll be right, mate,' cut in Max. He wrenched open the back door of his vehicle and tossed Simon a folded canvas tent. His actions were so rough that the Englishman grunted as he caught the heavy bundle. 'Do us a favour and set this up somewhere,' Max ordered. 'I'll look after the rest.'

He gathered up Mollie's equipment and headed for

the homestead. Gemma hurried after him, Mollie in her arms. 'I hope you're not going to spoil this evening by being rude to Simon,' she hissed through gritted teeth.

'Wouldn't dream of it,' he replied.

'Huh!' Gemma huffed. 'You almost winded him when you flung that heavy tent in his stomach.'

Max stopped in his tracks and stared at Gemma. With his spare hand, he pushed his broad-brimmed hat back and scratched his head. 'For crying out loud, Gemma. The man's out here to be toughened up. Of course he can catch a tent without flinching. How on earth do you think he manages to stay on a bucking horse or throw a bullock?'

Gemma's upper lip curled. 'I'm not talking about Simon's strength or lack of it. I'm talking about *your* behaviour. You just remember to mind your manners.'

'There's nothing wrong with my manners.'

'Let's hope not. I'd appreciate it if you were nice to my partner this evening. That way we'll all be able to have a pleasant time.'

He grunted. 'You'll be very sweet to Helena, of course.'

'Of course.'

Their hostess Ruth Neville greeted them with excited hugs and showed them where to set up Mollie's cot. By the time that was organised, the sun was almost set and guests, dressed in their finery, were starting to drift out of the homestead and out of the tents to gather on the lawn.

'Better get into our party clobber,' Max said. 'Let's hope the Pommy Jackaroo has the tent up. Do you want to get changed first?'

'No. You two fellows will be faster than me,' Gemma replied quickly.

While the men changed, she sat on the cool creek bank and tried to concentrate on the tranquillity of the bush and the creek below, but, to her annoyance, her imagination kept intruding, seriously disturbing her quest for peace and inner calm. No matter how hard she tried, she couldn't eliminate the pictures of Max that kept flashing through her mind. She tried to focus on Simon, her neat and personable partner.

Instead, Gemma found tempting visions taunting her… Visions of Max, only metres away, dressing inside the tent. She could picture his strong brown back and tightly toned buttocks as he shed his jeans and work shirt… The play of muscles in his chest as he raised his arms to haul a clean shirt over his head…the sideways jerking movement of his neck as he did up the tiny button at his collar and knotted his tie.

She had never seen Max do any of these things, so it was entirely disconcerting that her imagination could present such clear and detailed pictures.

'All done, Gemma. Your turn.'

The men emerged from the tent. Two handsome fellows looking their dashing best in sleek dark suits with gleaming white shirts and elegant black bow ties. Gemma smiled at Simon and tried to stifle any sense of comparison. Who cared if Max was taller, darker, broader-shouldered or had bluer eyes and a fuller, sexier mouth?

Simon was nice-looking, charming and polite—the kind of gentleman her mother had told her to look out for—the perfect partner for such an enchanting evening.

'You both look absolutely splendid,' she told them as she scrambled to her feet, and she sent Simon another encouraging smile.

'Don't take too long,' Max urged. 'We're getting thirsty.'

'I don't mind waiting for Gemma if you want to go ahead, Max,' Simon offered.

'No,' came the abrupt reply, accompanied by a frown. 'We may as well all go up together.'

As she slipped into the tent, Gemma grinned back at them. 'I don't have any problem zips, so I won't need any help with changing.'

'We weren't getting our hopes up,' Max drawled in reply.

Without a full-length mirror, Gemma had to hope that her dress was straight. The men had left a small lantern burning in a corner of the tent, and as darkness was encroaching very swiftly she needed its light to help her apply make-up while she peered into the minuscule mirror of her compact.

Given the limitations of her situation, she found complicated make-up difficult, but she was determined to make her appearance more dramatic than her usual casual look. Quickly she applied eye-shadow, mascara, a dusting of blush on her cheeks and lipstick. There wasn't much more she could do with her short, dark hair than run a little styling mousse through it with her fingers, so that it separated into feathery wisps.

Finally, she was satisfied and she slipped out of the tent. 'Hope I haven't taken too long.'

The men had been standing with their backs to her, looking at something on the far side of the creek. As she called to them they turned simultaneously and she felt self-conscious standing there before them in her new, dramatic, softly clinging gown.

Simon grinned broadly. 'My goodness,' he breathed. 'You look absolutely gorgeous.'

Max gave a very good impression of someone who had been shot by a stun gun. The shocked expression on his face sent Gemma's heart thumping and her knees to water. She reached for one of the tent's guy ropes to steady herself.

To her relief, he seemed to recover in a moment or two, but he walked towards her, smiling a strange, sadly lopsided little smile. 'We're waiting for Gemma Brown. Have you seen her?'

Gemma felt dizzy when he looked at her like that. She wondered how on earth he expected her to answer. 'She ran away with a gypsy,' she whispered and, blinking back silly tears, she dashed past Max to Simon.

Looping her arm through the Englishman's, she beamed up at him. 'Let's party, Mr Fox!'

'At once, Miss Brown!'

The trio crossed the stretch of paddock between the creek and the homestead and joined the revellers. A tall, willowy woman with auburn hair drawn back into a neat chignon separated from one of the groups and seemed to glide towards them, her pale, slender arms extended to Max.

Helena Roberts-Jones.

Dressed in an elegant cream chiffon gown and draped in pearls. Her attire toned perfectly with her titian colouring. 'Max, darling.'

'Helena.'

They embraced with a gentle, refined hug.

'So glad you were able to get away at last.'

'Yes,' Helena replied. 'I sent up a very demanding prayer—more of an order, really. No babies are allowed to be born tonight. No one's allowed to get appendicitis—or any other kind of illness, for that matter.'

'I'm sure no one would dare,' Max reassured her.

With a hand at her elbow, he turned her to meet Gemma and Simon.

'Oh,' Helena said when she was introduced to Gemma. 'So you're the young lady I spoke to on the phone—the nanny who's been staying with Max.' Her eyes widened. 'You sounded younger on the phone.'

'She usually *looks* much younger, too,' Max commented dryly.

'Oh, well,' shrugged Helena with a self-conscious little laugh, 'it's amazing what can be done with make-up.'

Gemma didn't appreciate Helena's attempt at a snub, but she had to admit that Max's partner was beautiful and exceedingly elegant. How good Helena and Max look together, she thought with an unexpected pang of dismay.

But this was not jealousy! She couldn't possibly be jealous. She didn't care what kind of women Max dated. It was wonderful that he and Helena were perfect for each other. They looked like people in an advertisement for something expensive—an exclusive restaurant, perhaps. He was the ruggedly handsome, worldly wise man and she his beautiful, steady, capable wife.

A girl approached their group with a tray of champagne cocktails and they all took a slim glass flute and toasted each other. Soon people from other groups, mainly friends from neighbouring properties, joined their little circle and more introductions were made. Several people who had known Gemma when she was growing up in the district greeted her as an old friend. A silver platter of delicious savouries came their way.

Night fell swiftly and completely while Gemma and Simon discussed stock horses with a cattleman who had travelled all the way from Julia Creek. The lights in the trees and the floodlights for the dance area came on, creating dazzling spots of colour and intimate shadowy areas around the garden.

An old friend Gemma had known since schooldays claimed her, and by the time she glanced back to where Max and Helena had been standing, they had disappeared.

After a time, Simon walked towards her. 'Would you like to dance?'

She looked across to the makeshift dance floor. Only a few couples were gyrating to taped music. She preferred to dance on a crowded floor.

'Apparently the band should be here by now,' Simon explained. 'I think Max has gone down the track a bit to see if they made it across the creek.'

'Helena went with him?' Gemma couldn't help asking.

'I'm not sure.' Simon took her hand and led her to the dance floor.

He held her companionably close without any tasteless groping and he moved smoothly in time to the music, guiding her expertly around the floor. Gemma couldn't help admiring Simon. He was one of those rare gems—a capable, resilient worker in the bush and a socially adept gentleman. She wished she felt more excited to be with him.

After the first bracket of songs finished, they stood together on the dance floor waiting for someone to change the tape. 'You're looking very beautiful tonight, Gemma. The belle of the ball, I'm sure.'

'Thank you.' She accepted his praise with a slight bow of her head and wished that his opinion meant more to her.

When the music started up again, there was a little

cheer from the crowd on the dance floor. It was a slow romantic number and once more Simon took her in his arms.

'Do you mind being labelled the Pommy Jackaroo?' she asked.

He laughed. 'I was a bit taken aback at first, but I know now that it's used with grudging respect. It means I may be a bit wet behind the ears—'

'But you're still a likeable sort of bloke.'

He looked into her eyes, as if searching for an answer to a question he hadn't asked. 'Something like that.' After a few more laps around the floor, he asked, 'I understand you grew up in these parts?'

'Yes, that's right.'

'But you don't talk about it much.'

Gemma grimaced. 'Everyone around here knows my life story. You can't keep any secrets in the outback.'

He smiled. 'I've discovered that.'

They swirled past another dancing couple.

'So you already know all about me?'

He looked a trifle embarrassed and slowed his pace till they were merely shuffling together. 'I know that everyone in the district expected you to pair up with Max's kid brother Dave, but you didn't. And now you're back here with his daughter.'

'My goodness,' Gemma groaned. 'When you put it like that it sounds highly suspect, doesn't it?'

She quickly explained that she and Dave had never been serious and told him about Dave and Isobel in Africa, and she was startled by the relief that shone in Simon's eyes when he heard her version of the situation. His hand at her waist tightened its hold and Gemma drew in her breath to keep her body from touching his. She stared sadly at the star-studded sky over his shoulder and knew with a terrible certainty that tonight wasn't going to be the dazzling evening she had hoped for.

The setting had all the right ingredients. Above them arched the huge outback sky, like an enormous dome lined with black velvet and studded with diamonds. Every so often, the familiar, heartwarming call of black cockatoos came floating up from the trees along the creek. All around them happy, hard-working people were enjoying one of the rare opportunities life in the bush afforded to dress up to the nines, kick up one's heels and have a good time.

This should be a night to remember. She wanted so much to enjoy herself with Simon.

But she had run slap bang into her same old, same old problem...

It didn't seen to matter how many likeable and charming men she met. When they got interested in her and their ideas turned to romance, she wanted to back off.

The bracket of songs finished, and Gemma opted for another drink. Simon fetched it for her and they went to join a group sitting at a table near the sunken fish pond. A little fountain played in the middle of the pond, its soft splashing sounds making a comforting backdrop. But Simon sat close beside her with an arm draped over her shoulders and several times, as they chatted, she found him looking at her, an intense spark burning in his eyes.

She set her glass down on the table. 'I'd like to go and check on Mollie,' she murmured, and, stood quickly. She hurried away before he could reply. Across the lawn she sped, holding her dress away from the dew-covered grass.

In the bedroom off the side verandah, Mollie was sleeping like an angel, but Gemma stayed watching over her for some time. There was a soft night-light in the room and she could see the little golden head, the thick dark lashes lying against her soft cheeks, one pink star-fish hand resting on top of the patchwork quilt and the other cuddling a tiny pink rabbit. What a darling little girl she was.

It occurred to Gemma that she was doing rather a good job of looking after Isobel and Dave's baby—and she was enjoying it, too. That was totally unexpected. She leaned across the cot and whispered a prayer for the safety of little Mollie's parents and she wondered if she would ever have a baby of her own. Not if she continued to run away from every man who ever looked twice at her, she thought with a sigh.

A mirror on the opposite wall caught her attention. She saw the reflection of her lovely gown and couldn't help admiring its colour—the pale, silvery blue of moon-light. As she stared at the mirror she saw a dark shape move behind her on the verandah. But there was no sound and she reasoned that it must have been a shrub being blown by the wind.

But a second later she was gripping the railing of Mollie's cot with a shaking hand.

Images of a shadowy figure…a pale, blue dress and…a darkened verandah…dropped into her mind as if some-body was slipping slides into a projector.

Déjà vu.

It had happened before.

This scene, these images… A party on a night like this…a dress this colour…

And the photograph Max still kept on the dressing table in her room.

CHAPTER SIX

GEMMA slid her arms along the cot's wooden railing until her fingers interlaced. She lowered her burning face to rest on her hands. Every detail of the memory of that night replayed once more in her mind. Piece by relentless piece.

Five years earlier, when she was eighteen, she had come home from university for Dave's twenty-first birthday party. The Jardines had invited nearly everyone in the district to a huge celebration at the Goodbye Creek homestead.

That evening Gemma had had the time of her life in her lovely new dress—her first formal evening gown—pale blue with tiny straps, a figure-hugging bodice and a dreamy, floating skirt.

It had been a hot night, but she had danced and danced in her new silver sandals and drunk rather too much champagne. She'd stood by Dave as he'd cut his birthday cake and, in front of all the guests, he had kissed her. This had been greeted by a rousing chorus of cheers and loud cat-calls. And, while his father had made a speech, Dave had flung a possessive arm around her shoulders.

By midnight, after she'd given every second dance to Dave and divided up the others between the eager young men from the district, Gemma had been exhausted and just a little dizzy. When the band had finally stopped for a well-earned break, she had been relieved that her dancing partner, the head stockman from Acacia Downs, was happy to rejoin his mates around the beer keg. Gemma had dashed away to hunt down some cool lemonade and a quiet spot to catch her breath.

She had found just what she needed at one end of the verandah, an old rattan lounge chair lined with ancient patchworked cushions and screened from the party by a vine-covered lattice. Gratefully she'd collapsed into it, flinging one leg over the chair's arm while she sipped her icy lemonade and not caring one jot that it was an unladylike pose. Hot and sticky, she had tried to fan herself with her hand.

'Oh, boy,' she murmured softly. 'What a great party.'

She wondered where Dave had got to, but wasn't too worried. There were so many people about; he could be anywhere. The ice clinked as she drained the lemonade and she placed the glass on the wooden floor beside her. Releasing a deep sigh of satisfaction, she slipped off her sandals and wriggled her aching feet. Already she was feeling much better.

A soft sound behind her brought her curling around in the chair to peer into the shadows.

Someone was there. A man, leaning against the verandah railing and, like her, enjoying a moment of peace. She was sure she recognised the familiar silhouette.

'Dave?'

The answer reached her soft and low from the shadows. 'Hi, Gemma.'

In a flash, she was out of the chair and closing the distance between them. Standing high on her bare toes, she threw her arms around his neck and dropped a carefree, happy little kiss on his lips.

Of course, he kissed her back.

And she knew at that moment this man wasn't Dave.

She should have pulled away! Of course she should have. Especially when the dreadful truth dawned.

The man she was kissing was Max.

But a part of her, some dreadful, shameless part of her, didn't care! From the moment Max's mouth landed hotly on hers Gemma couldn't help herself. His kiss was so exciting, so intensely arousing, all she worried about was that he might stop.

She felt as if she'd stepped through a door straight into womanhood. She didn't know if it was the champagne or the hot night, the moonlight, or a taste of midnight madness, but in a heartbeat she and Max were exchanging kisses more breathtaking than anything she'd experienced before. Kissing Dave had been nice, but now something seriously sexy was happening.

She had no idea tasting and touching could drive her so wild. His mouth was hot and demanding as his tongue sought hers, making ripple after ripple of shocking, heated pleasure flood through her. For the first time in her life she knew why people made so much fuss about making love.

At first she looped her hands around his neck, but soon they were straying restlessly through his thick hair and across his shoulders, and, under her seeking fingers, she could feel the roll and flex of his hard muscles as he tugged her closer.

Then his hands began to move. Her skin sizzled as slowly, lazily, he made teasing trails from her waist, up her sides to her breasts. Cascades of sensation streamed through her and she heard a soft moan drifting from her lips.

Next moment she was pushing her breasts into the willing heat of his hands, wishing she could tear away the filmy fabric of her gown. It didn't matter that this man usually regarded her with disdain. Right now, she didn't want anything between her skin and his daring touch. An astonishing, warm and pulsing hunger fanned through her. And she realised that she wanted to give herself to him. Wanted him to possess her completely.

Willed him to take her.

'Oh, please, please,' she whispered.

He gave a gruff cry of protest, but still held her close, burying his face in her neck.

Having no experience and very little skill, Gemma responded purely by instinct, urging him with her body to understand her need. This astonishing need she'd never felt before. Boldly, she pressed herself into him, standing on tiptoe to nudge his lower body with hers, thrusting her swelling breasts against him, taking his face between her hands and covering his mouth and jaw with more eager, hungry kisses. 'Please make love to me.'

'Oh, God.' Max went very still. His harsh breaths as he dragged air into his lungs were the only indication he hadn't turned to stone. 'I'm so sorry, Gemma.'

At the sound of his voice the spell was broken—shattered into a thousand accusations.

Shaking, Gemma backed away from him, her hands tightly clasped at the neckline of her dress.

In stunned disbelief at what she'd done, she watched as Max raised an arm and drew it across his forehead, as if trying to clear his brain of what had just happened.

She was dazed, numb with shock, unable to speak.

How could she have done all that? With Max?

He was still in darkness, so she couldn't see the expression on his face, but she could see the slump in his shoulders, and the way his head hung low. She could tell that he was as horrified as she was by what they'd just shared.

The tears came as she edged further away from him. Her vision blurred so that his dark form swam against the night sky. *How on earth had it happened?* She'd been in darkened corners with Dave before now and she'd never behaved like that.

Dave had never been like that!

This knowledge was too awful to bear. It sent her scurrying down the verandah, without stopping for her sandals. She ran into her bedroom and stayed in the silent house for the rest of the night, while the party continued outside.

When Dave came looking for her, Gemma pretended to be asleep. She wanted to tell him what had happened, to say that it was a mistake, that she was sorry. But the admission was too terrible. The words remained locked in her throat.

So instead of unburdening her guilt when Dave stood in her doorway, she closed her eyes and made her breathing regular and deep. After some time, she heard his footsteps echo as they moved away down the verandah and into the warm night.

She would never speak about what had happened to anyone.

The next morning Dave expressed puzzlement over her early departure from the party and she told him she'd had a headache from too much champagne. After that little lie, there was no way she could try to explain what had really happened. In the daylight, it seemed even harder to understand how she could ever have allowed herself to behave like that.

And, of course, she could never bring herself to speak to Max about it.

For the next few days, he was away on some remote part of the property. 'Checking boundaries,' someone told her.

Two days later, just before she returned to the city, a slightly nervous Dave asked her if they could 'have a bit of a chat' and the outcome was his suggestion that perhaps he and Gemma shouldn't feel too committed to each other just because they'd been friends since forever.

Her guilty heart reacted wildly. *Had Max spoken to Dave?*

But he seemed to be thinking on a different tangent. 'I know everyone around here has always expected that one day we'd be a couple, but, hell, Gemma, I'm sorry, but I think we maybe need some space—a chance to meet a few more people.'

Once she got over the shock of Dave's suggestion, Gemma adjusted to it rather quickly.

Dave continued, 'You see, we're only young, and I'm not sure we've got everything happening the way it's supposed to for people who eventually get hitched. Maybe we never will.'

She looked hard at him then, and realised that a part of her had always known she and Dave could never be more than friends. 'I know what you mean,' she whispered, and her cheeks flamed as she remembered the shameful way she'd behaved in Max's arms.

'You're sure you understand?' he asked, his sense of relief making his eyes shine.

'There's supposed to be more than friendship—something a bit more—cataclysmic.'

'Cata-what?' Dave sounded puzzled, but then he grinned ruefully. 'You mean fireworks, the earth moving—that sort of thing?'

Suddenly embarrassed, Gemma simply nodded.

Dave leaned over and brushed her cheek affection-ately with his knuckles. 'We've been the very best of mates, Gem. I'm sure we always will be.'

She was surprised how easily she'd got used to the idea of parting with Dave but, although she'd learned a thing or two about 'chemistry' on the night of the party, she couldn't let herself think that this willingness to sep-arate from one brother had anything to do with how she felt about the other.

Max returned to the homestead the afternoon before she was to go back to Brisbane and he tried, just once, to speak to her.

She was taking a final walk along the tree-shaded track by the creek and had stopped to sit on a flat granite boulder to watch electric-blue dragonflies chase each other across the sunlit water. The sound of a twig snap-ping alerted her that someone was coming, and when she looked up she saw Max's tall figure striding towards her through the trees.

Alarmed, she jumped to her feet, and was poised for flight when his voice reached her.

'Gemma!'

Her face flamed with embarrassment and she felt sick.

'Gemma,' he called again, his long strides bringing him very close now. 'We need to talk.'

She didn't want to speak to him, couldn't bear to dis-cuss that kiss. Talking about it would only make every-thing they had done all too shamefully real. The horrid truth, that she had offered herself in a wild fit of passion to Max, of all people, was terrifying. She couldn't deal with it.

She wouldn't let him near.

Running away felt foolish, but Gemma had to flee that

scene. Like a hunted rabbit she darted off, not following the track, but ducking and diving through the undergrowth. To her relief, Max didn't follow her. She imagined it was beneath his dignity to scramble after her through the scratchy acacia scrub and lantana.

By the time she reached the homestead, breathless and panting, she'd decided that the only way she could ever face the rest of her life was to behave as if the incident had never happened.

She'd done her best to keep that memory locked away ever since. In her mind she'd pictured herself forcing the regrettable interlude into an ugly little padlocked box, and whenever it tried to haunt her she would visualise the lid snapping tight and the fat key turning in the lock, holding the horrible memory inside. And for long stretches of time it had worked. She'd been able to forget about the kiss and get on with her life. But every so often the memory caught her by surprise.

Like tonight…when once more she wore a dress of pale, pale blue and knew that, behind her, a man waited in the dark.

Gemma raised her head and the shadowy shape on the verandah behind her moved. She watched the reflection in the mirror and saw Max step forward until he was framed by the doorway. A wall light outside made his dark hair shine, but cast shadows lower on his face. Hardly daring to breathe, she remained very still with her back to him.

'Everything OK?' he asked softly, coming closer. He stopped just behind her, looking over her shoulder at the sleeping baby girl.

She turned, ever so slightly, in his direction. 'She's sleeping like an angel,' she whispered.

He was so close she could feel his warmth at her back, the stirring of his breath against her hair when he murmured, 'She's cute, isn't she?'

His hand touched her bare shoulder and she jumped.

'Come outside,' he said close to her ear.

Knowing she couldn't spend the rest of the evening watching a baby sleep, she followed him—after a slight hesitation. As she did, she sent up a frantic prayer that, after all these years, Max had forgotten that terrible incident.

On the verandah again, he paused, and she was so nervous she rushed to speak, to fill in the moments that must follow with safe, harmless chatter. 'Did you find the band?'

'Yes.' He cocked his head in the direction of the party. 'They're a group of townies and so they're not used to driving in the bush. They tried to take that bend just before the creek far too quickly and their van ended up in a ditch.'

'Goodness—was anyone hurt?'

'No, they were very lucky. The singer has a sprained wrist, but Helena's attending to it.'

'Poor Helena. She hasn't been able to keep her night free of medical duties after all.'

'She's used to it.'

'Will they still play for the dancing?'

'Sure. They're setting up now.'

'Great,' she said, extra brightly. She stepped quickly away from him. 'Then let's go. We'd better find our partners and dance the night away with them.'

'Hold it, Gemma.' His hand reached out and caught hers.

Just like that—her fingers were linked with his. Such

a flimsy trap and yet, for the life of her, she couldn't pull away. 'What—do you want?' The words felt squeezed from her throat.

'I want to tell you how lovely you look tonight.'

The moon, spilling through the shubbery, illuminated his face and Gemma saw a startling tenderness that made her want to weep.

'Thank you,' she whispered.

'Are you enjoying yourself?'

'Of course. I'm having the time of my life. It's a wonderful party.'

He gave her a look that said he didn't believe her, but he grinned anyway and said, 'Glad you're having a good time. It would be a pity to waste this stunning dress.' He touched her skin, just above the sloping neckline of her gown, and she was sure her heart stilled.

In the burning silence, he whispered, 'You've grown up, Gem.'

Tears welled in her throat, making it hard to reply. 'What—what did you expect?'

'Oh, I expected something quite spectacular.' The skin around his eyes creased as he smiled.

This conversation was dangerous, but she was mesmerised by his voice, deep, yet rough around the edges, as if his throat felt as choked as hers. She couldn't drag herself away, despite the embarrassing memories still hot in her thoughts.

As if sensing her confusion, Max took both her hands in his and pulled her towards him. 'Now that you're so grown-up, I think it's time we talked about a little matter that we should have discussed long ago—five years ago.'

'No, Max, no!' She hated the sudden note of panic in her voice.

'The night of Dave's twenty-first.'

'Don't do this,' she pleaded, trying to pull her hands from his.

This was exactly what mustn't happen. Remembering was one thing, but she couldn't talk about that night now any more easily than she could then. It was much better to go on pretending they'd both forgotten.

The light in his eyes dimmed. 'You're frightened?'

She gave a tiny nod and looked away, unable to meet the directness of his gaze. 'It's not worth dredging up the past, Max.'

'You don't want to hear my apology?'

'*Your* apology?' *He thought he was to blame?* Through brimming tears, she dragged her eyes back to meet his.

'Hell, Gemma, don't sound so surprised. I knew exactly who was in my arms that night, but you thought it was Dave. I deceived you and I've had to live with the weight of that deception all these years. I cheated you *and* my brother.'

'Oh, Max.' She couldn't stop the tears from flowing and she lunged forward. His strong arms come round her and she sank against him, burying her face in his chest.

'Damn it,' he murmured as he stroked the back of her neck. 'I've been worried sick that you'd been traumatised by this whole business.'

The full-blown remorse she heard in his voice shocked her. On that night all those years ago, when her sense of guilt had coiled through her like a hissing, striking serpent, she hadn't stopped to consider that Max might be feeling guilty. She had always been quite certain that she was the evil one. She was the sinner.

Far worse than Eve in the Garden of Eden.

The biblical Eve had simply held out a piece of fruit

to Adam, but Gemma had hurled herself into Max's arms, rubbed her body all over him and pleaded with him to make love to her.

Oh, Lord.

And now he was claiming the guilt. When all along she'd known it was Max she was kissing...

In the distant garden, a guitarist from the band twanged a few notes and she could hear the singer clearing his throat into the mike. 'One, two, three, testing...testing...'

As these ordinary, familiar sounds reached her from the party, from the ordinary, familiar world beyond the verandah, Gemma felt she was emerging from a dream. It was as if everything that had happened in her life so far had been leading her to this point and as if her entire future might well be shaped by her next move.

It was time to be honest with Max.

She knew that if she were as adult as Max assumed her to be she would let him off the hook. Any mature woman in her situation would admit that she'd known exactly which brother she was kissing that night, and then she might even let him know that she was quite interested in kissing him again and see what he had to say about that.

That was probably what most well-adjusted women would do.

Or she could play the part of the outraged virgin, grudgingly accepting his apology while struggling out of his arms.

That would be childish and deceitful but, then again, she'd practised being a coward for five years now.

Or there was one other way...

CHAPTER SEVEN

LIFTING her face from his dampened shirt front, Gemma swiped at her tears and sniffed. 'For heaven's sake, Max,' she began in a shaky, high-pitched voice. 'Don't torture yourself with a guilt trip about some little old kiss that happened five years ago. That's ancient history. I haven't been worrying about it. I haven't given it a moment's thought.'

'You haven't?' He looked so disbelieving she found it hard to meet his gaze. His hand reached out and with his fingertips he touched her wet cheek. 'If that's so, why all these tears?' His attempt at a laugh fell short of the mark. 'And why do I look like I've spilled drink all down my shirt?'

'I'm sorry about that,' she said, seeing the damage her tears and her mascara had done. 'I'll get something to mop you up.' She turned, about to dash away, but he grabbed her arm and swung her back.

'Hey, not so fast, Gemma Brown.'

And she wished, oh, how she wished that she wasn't back so close to him again. Any minute now she would be doing a repeat performance—reaching up on her tiptoes, throwing her arms around Max Jardine's neck and kissing him till morning. Her stomach flipped at the thought.

She forced the tremors out of her voice. 'You had something else you wanted to say?'

His sad and thoughtful expression as his gaze rested on her made her feel he understood more about what she hadn't been saying than what she'd actually said. Eventually, he broke the silence. 'So that was just some little old kiss, was it?'

Her palms were sweating and, instinctively, she rubbed them down her thighs, but when his gaze lingered there, she hastily clasped her hands in front of her. 'I'm surprised that a man who has, at the very least, *three* women currently panting after him, would give one little kiss a second thought.'

He emitted a strange little grunt, and a moment later his hands were gripping her shoulders, holding her squarely in front of him. His eyes glinted fiercely. 'What if I *have* thought about that night—more than once or twice? What if I think we should try to lay this ghost?' His head dipped closer and she felt dizzy with longing. 'How about we try that little old kiss again, Gemma, and you can show me that I'm forgiven?'

Gemma's heartbeats thundered in her ears. Her weak and foolish body wanted to be in Max's arms again and to experience that passionate mouth locked with hers! But she couldn't bear to make a fool of herself again. 'There—there's nothing to forgive,' she stammered.

'That's not what your tears tell me.' His lips lowered to kiss her bare shoulder and, in spite of her caution, Gemma arched her neck sideways, offering an inviting path for him to follow all the way to her mouth. Already her senses anticipated the moment when his lips reached hers.

'I'm so glad you've grown up, Gemma,' he murmured, his breath hot against her skin. 'You smell wonderful. Feel so womanly, so soft.'

Oh, Lord. His mouth was too close. She needed him.

'Five years is a long time between kisses,' he whispered.

And at that moment she discovered just how immature and unsophisticated she still was. While her body
yearned to be seduced, her mind succumbed to panic.

'Max, wait a minute.' Pushing against his chest with
both hands, she broke his hold and stepped back. 'This
is—this is all wrong!'

His hands rose in a gesture of helplessness. 'It feels
all wrong to you?'

One part of her wanted to admit that being in his arms
felt every kind of wonderful, but instead she rattled off
a string of desperate excuses. 'It doesn't matter how it
feels. I know it's wrong. You don't love me.' Her voice
broke a little to make that admission, but she hurried on.
'I'm sorry if you got the wrong impression about me
five years ago. I'm not free and easy with my—with
my—'

Her eyes fixed on his exquisite mouth and for a
breathless moment she couldn't continue, couldn't remember exactly what she was protesting about. She
struggled to focus on the world beyond this verandah—
the guests in the garden, the sleeping baby nearby. 'The
point is—I came out here at your insistence to look after
Mollie, not to be your—your mistress.'

'Mistress?' he repeated, his brows frowning low over
amused eyes.

'Yes.'

'Your imagination's running away on you, Gemma.
There's a hell of a jump from one little kiss to...ev-
erything a mistress has to offer.'

Oh, Lord! And didn't she know it? It was a jump
she'd never made. Fierce blushes burned in her cheeks.
His words embarrassed her, angered her, *hurt* her!
Smouldering, Gemma drew further away, wrenching her
shoulders back and pointing in the direction of the party.

'That's exactly why you should get back out there to Helena.'

He remained standing before her in silence, as if he needed time to adjust to what she was saying.

'How can you kiss me when Helena's waiting?'

'That's a very good question.' Max watched her face carefully. 'Think about it.'

But she couldn't think about it. Not when her brain was seized by mind-numbing confusion. 'And Simon will be dreadfully worried about me. Any minute now he'll turn up here looking for me. How can you think about kissing me again? This is just as bad as last time. Don't forget I came to this ball at the invitation of another man.'

'Huh,' muttered Max. 'Of course, we wouldn't want His British Highness to find you in a compromising clinch.'

'Certainly not!' she hissed. 'And if you're any sort of a man—any sort of *gentleman*—you wouldn't have tried this a second time!'

He let out a loud, weary sigh. 'You're so right. You'd better get back to the party.'

'I intend to.'

As she turned to go, he called, 'So, Gemma, have we sorted things out?'

She looked back at him over her shoulder as he stood there with an arm outstretched, and it took all her will power not to run back and have him hold her again.

'You're fine about—about everything?'

'Absolutely everything, Max.'

She turned quickly again before the stupid tears threatened and she hurried down the steps into the garden. Never had she felt so confused—bewildered by her own feelings and by Max's behaviour. How could he want to dally with her and exchange a few kisses when he had Helena waiting nearby?

Think about it, he'd said. But what conclusion could she come to other than the fact that Max could kiss any number of women at the drop of a hat? Did he fancy himself as some kind of outback Don Juan?

Grateful for the subdued lighting in the garden, she dabbed at her wet face with a handkerchief and, as she threaded her way through the laughing guests, she vowed to find the Pommy Jackaroo and be very, very nice to him for the rest of the evening.

The band, eager to make up for lost time, played loudly and energetically into the early hours of the morning. Their singer, thanks to Helena's expert attention, seemed to have recovered from his ordeal and crooned seductively while nursing his arm in a sling.

Gemma danced with Simon, or sat with him and listened to his stories about adjusting to the life in the outback, and, once or twice, she allowed him to kiss her. They were very nice kisses. Like Simon himself. Skilful, practised, not too demanding—and yet hinting that he would be keen to demand a great deal more if she showed the right response.

When Gemma couldn't dredge up the appropriate response, she felt very depressed. Her partner remained charming and polite. But as the evening wore on, pretending to be even vaguely interested in him became more and more difficult.

And there were only so many times she could check on Mollie as an excuse to get away.

When she wasn't dancing, Gemma tried desperately to avoid watching Helena in Max's arms as they glided elegantly around the dance floor, but she didn't miss the touching moments of intimacy the other couple shared. She saw how Helena dropped her head onto Max's broad shoulder as they danced and the way she smiled up into his eyes as if she adored him. And she noted the possessive way Max held her close, his hand cradling her sleek hip. *The two-timing rat!*

As Gemma sat watching the dancers and twisting the stem of her champagne flute between anxious fingers, she reflected guiltily on her feeble response to Simon's romantic efforts. It was the same pattern all over again. The same sense of something missing that had dogged all her relationships with men.

She caught sight of Max's rugged profile dipping courteously towards Helena as she whispered something in his ear.

And suddenly Gemma was shaking, feeling ill, as a terrible realisation flooded her thoughts. She tried to hold back the knowledge that pounded in her head. *My dilemma is Max's fault. I've been in love with him for five years.*

Damn his sexy eyes!

Every man she'd met, since that night five years ago, had only been able to offer a pale shadow of what Max had given her. His kisses and caresses had stirred and aroused her beyond her wildest imaginings. Dave had simply been the first in a series of young men who had found a disappointing response when they'd tried to kiss Gemma.

And it was all because of Max.

He had given her a taste of a different kind of loving.

And, by doing so when he had no real interest in her except as someone to tease and spar with, he had wrecked her chances of happiness.

From beneath wet lashes, she stole another surreptitious glance at Max and Helena. They had stopped dancing and were laughing over a joke told by their host, Tom Neville. Helena's arm was draped casually around Max's neck and she nestled her beautifully groomed head against him. When she laughed, she buried her face in his chest.

Gemma dragged her gaze elsewhere, before she made a fool of herself by crying openly. It was so painful to finally accept the fact that after she'd tasted Max's brand of lovemaking *she* had never been satisfied with anyone else.

But if she wanted him now, she would have to take her place in the line-up beside a string of other women.

By one a.m., Gemma couldn't take any more. She was too emotionally drained to keep pretending enjoyment and too exhausted to dance another step, so she flopped back into another chair and smiled apologetically at Simon. 'I'm absolutely pooped,' she told him. 'And I know Mollie is going to wake at the crack of dawn, so I'm going to call it a night.'

He jumped to his feet. 'I'll walk you down to the tent.'

'Thank you.' An expectant gleam in his eyes made her hesitate. 'Um—don't rush, Simon. I'll make one final check on Mollie first.'

Feeling foolish, she dashed towards the homestead again. To her left, she could see a couple of teenagers emerging from the darkness at the edge of the lawn, the boy swaggered slightly and the girl was trying to look super-cool as she combed tousled hair with her fingers. They seemed to take a little fumble in the shadows in their stride. Was she the only person who remained scarred for life by that kind of experience?

'Gemma.'

As she reached the foot of the stairs, Max's voice

called from behind. She hesitated, not sure if she could face him again, but eventually she turned around.

He was alone. Tall, dark, handsome in his debonair tuxedo, and alone. In the moonlight, his hair looked soft and exceedingly touchable. Gemma clenched her fists as if to ward off his spellbinding impact.

'Are you going back to the tent now?' he asked.

'Yes,' she replied coldly. *Did he have to check on her every move?* She couldn't help snapping back with, 'What's it to you?'

Max cleared his throat. 'My things are in the tent,' he said, glaring at her as if she were planning a string of shocking crimes. 'Could you toss my swag and my clothes out before you and, er—the Pommy Jackaroo— I'm sorry, you and *Simon* settle in there?'

Highly embarrassed, she let her eyes dart away.

'I presume you two want the tent to yourselves,' Max drawled. His words were accompanied by a loud yawn, as if he found the whole subject tedious.

'N-no,' she stammered. 'Don't worry about that.'

'Don't worry about what, exactly?'

Gemma was sure he was being deliberately obtuse. 'We—Simon and I won't need the tent.'

'I beg your pardon?'

'We're not looking for privacy.'

'You won't be needing the tent to yourselves?'

She huffed out an angry sigh. 'You're not hard of hearing, Max. You heard me the first time.' Looking up at the cloudless night sky, she added, 'It's a beautiful night. We can sleep under the stars in our swags.' She forced a face-splitting smile his way. 'And leave the tent for you and Helena.'

To her surprise, his confident gaze dropped and, with his hands in his pockets, he shuffled his shiny black dress shoes in the dewy grass. 'Helena's been offered a comfortable bed up in the homestead.' He looked up again and grinned at her, a surprisingly shy grin. 'You know how highly respected doctors are in the bush. Her hostess can't let her rough it with the common folk.'

'Of course,' Gemma responded, and a silly little laugh escaped as she tried to cover her highly unsuitable sense of relief. 'I'm sure the poor darling's exhausted and needs her—her rest.' She hesitated. 'In that case, I guess we three can all share the tent.'

He looked startled by her suggestion. His throat worked. 'No, you're right. It's a clear night. I'd prefer to sleep under the stars myself.'

She followed his gaze up to the heavens. The silhouette of a huge bird, probably a tawny owl, was winging its way to the east, with the Southern Cross as its backdrop. Her comment came spontaneously. 'I love these big outback skies.'

'Yeah? I guess you'll miss them when you go back?' He looked unusually ill-at-ease, as if this was a question he hadn't meant to ask.

'Definitely.' She nodded and wrapped her arms around herself, wishing he would leave her.

Standing here with him again—alone—she felt far too vulnerable. She dropped her gaze, afraid that if he looked into her eyes he would discover the bitter home truths she'd had to face up to this evening.

She didn't want him to guess the awesome power he had over her.

For another thirty seconds she hovered on the bottom step, embarrassed and lost for words, and then she turned abruptly and hurried up the steps that led to Mollie's room.

'Just throw my things out of the tent anyway,' Max

called after her. 'I might see this party through till dawn yet... And, Gemma?'

At the top of the steps she paused, but there was no way she could look back. She stood with her back rigid, but her ears were straining to catch his words.

His voice drifted up to her, low and gentle as a lullaby. 'Sleep tight.'

When she told Simon that she wanted to sleep outside, he was a little surprised and, she suspected, disappointed.

'That's what everyone does,' she replied with what she hoped passed for wide-eyed innocence. 'We get changed in the tents and use them for storage, but why waste a wonderful night stuck under canvas when you could be out here?' She flung her arms wide to take in the warm night, the silver-speckled sky, the creek bank and the bush beyond.

Simon scratched his head as he surveyed the scene. Other visitors were settling for the night. Some dark humps suggested people already asleep under the stars. In other areas people were sitting on their swags still chatting and laughing quietly. Further along the bank a group had lit a small camp fire and were gathered in a circle, spinning more yarns and tossing back more drinks. But from one or two tents nearby she could hear rustling, suppressed giggles and sultry murmurs. There was no doubting what was happening in there.

Simon stepped towards Gemma and said in a quiet voice, 'I had something a little cosier in mind.'

With her hands clasped in front of her, Gemma turned to face him. 'Not this time, Simon. But thank you for a lovely evening. I've thoroughly enjoyed myself.'

His face tightened. 'Do you really mean that?'

'Of course I do. I've never had a more charming or attentive escort. And there's absolutely no doubt that you can out-dance Aussie blokes.'

He was silent and she knew that he'd hoped to be more than her dancing partner. She saw a little flash of hurt in his eyes and, because she could offer him no comfort, she hurried into the tent to change before dragging her swag out onto the grass.

When she finally settled for sleep, Gemma was grateful for her emotional and physical exhaustion. To her surprise, she slept soundly and the next morning, although she was still very tired, she woke out of habit around dawn to find Max lying only a few metres away, curled on his side. She felt a familiar pain in her chest as she stole a secretive look at him sleeping there, his mouth open just a little, so she could hear the soft hush of his breathing. Simon was on the other side—sound asleep on his back with one hand flung over his eyes.

As quietly as she could, Gemma scrambled out of the swag and made her way down the bracken-covered bank to the creek where she planned to wash her face. White mist trailed softly over the surface of the water like a bridal veil. Early mornings were her favourite time in the bush. She perched at the water's edge, enjoying the almost spiritual silence broken every so often by the occasional lilting songs of magpies or the cheeky chatter of budgerigars and honeyeaters.

Dipping her hands into the chill, clear creek, she splashed her face. *Oh, Lord*, she thought as the refreshing water hit her cheeks. *I love it out here.* She tipped her head back and stared at the criss-cross of leafy green branches above her. Through them she could see patches of sky. Although it was early morning, the heavens were already bright blue—blue as Max's eyes.

I don't want to go back to Brisbane.

The thought bounced into her mind and wouldn't budge. The longer she sat there, the more she was sure of it. Ever since she'd come back, her heart had been remembering and absorbing the things she loved most about the bush and now it ached for this tough, uncivilised country. And this yearning had nothing to do with a certain tough, uncivilised cattleman.

She whispered a wish that she could stay.

So many times in her teens she'd paddled a canoe down this creek, sliding silently under the willow-like branches close to the dank, brown banks. Behind the curtain of green lace, she'd stayed in the shaded, totally private world for hours, watching till a water rat came slinking out of its home beneath the tangled roots of a paperbark. She would throw leaves and sticks onto the water, knowing such movements would bring black bream darting out from beneath logs to snap at the surface in the hope of finding a juicy insect. Sometimes a long-necked tortoise would poke its little head out of the water and stare at her with yellow eyes.

All her life she had known and loved this creek, this district. It was in her blood and the thought of leaving it again brought a pain like a heavy fist gripping tightly in her chest. The first time she'd left had been important. She'd needed to discover the world beyond this little corner of the outback. But now she'd been away and seen what the rest of the world had to offer, and suddenly she knew with absolute certainty this was where she wanted to be.

It made no sense, of course. Her work belonged in the city and she needed to get back there as soon as she could.

And, even more importantly, she needed to forget

about Max. Hanging around would only make things far worse—rub salt in the freshly opened wound.

With a sad sigh, Gemma turned away from the creek and, after slipping into the tent to tidy herself, she hurried up to the homestead, knowing there was every chance that Mollie would be awake by now. In the garden, there were several others up and about already and some stalwart party animals, who had obviously stayed up all night and were flopped in chairs in one corner, looking a touch the worse for wear. Their host was lighting the barbecue in preparation for the recovery breakfast and he gave Gemma a good-natured wave as she passed.

Mollie was wide awake when Gemma entered her room. Wide awake and beaming with a big surprise.

'Good heavens!' Gemma cried as she dashed towards the cot. 'Mollie, you clever little muffin! You're standing up!'

The baby gurgled at her, obviously very proud of herself as she stood, clinging to the cot railing and peering over the top. Gemma hugged her and smothered her with kisses. 'You clever, clever little girl. Fancy standing up all by yourself. Oh, what will Mummy and Daddy think? And Uncle Max?'

This news was too good to keep to herself. Gemma ran to the doorway. How weird that she should feel so madly excited! She had to fetch Max. 'Stay there, darling. Don't move!' she called to Mollie before racing along the verandah and flying across the lawn, down to the creek bank.

'Max! Max!' she called, but when her cries were met by groans from sleeping forms in nearby swags, she knelt beside him and shook his shoulder, whispering, 'Max! Wake up! Come and take a look at Mollie!'

'What's wrong?' Max shot out of the swag and shoved aside the tumble of hair in his eyes. 'Gemma! What is it?' Wearing nothing but jeans, he looked as wild and ready for action as a Hollywood hero.

'It's all right, Max.' Gemma touched his arm, but when he looked down at her hand on his skin, she drew back again. 'Mollie's standing up!'

He frowned as he took in her news. Then his jaw dropped. 'She is?' His face creased into a grin. 'That's fantastic!'

'Come and see for yourself.'

She tugged at his elbow.

Together they raced back to the homestead. Max took the steps two at a time and reached Mollie before Gemma but, to her relief, the baby was still performing her clever act, standing with her little hands clutching the rail and crowing proudly as she bobbed up and down on unsteady legs.

'What a little champion!' he laughed, skipping around the cot and looking proud as punch as if somehow he'd achieved this small miracle himself. He grinned smugly at Gemma. 'If she's true blue Jardine stock, we'll be watching her standing up today and riding a pony tomorrow.'

Gemma laughed. 'Give the poor girl a break.'

'No fear,' responded Max. 'We'll have her running to meet her parents.'

'Is everything all right?'

A cool voice in the doorway brought them swinging around. Helena, looking pale without her make-up, but ultra-elegant in a classically tailored white silk dressing gown, leaned against the door post and peered in at them uncertainly. 'There seemed to be a commotion.' Her eyes darted suspiciously from Max's half-dressed state to Gemma and back again.

'Just a little celebration,' Max explained. He stepped aside and made a deep bow, sweeping one arm in Mollie's direction like a ring master in a circus announcing the star act. 'Mollie Jardine has joined the rest of the human race. Drum roll, please. May I present one small lady, who is now *standing upright*!'

Helena looked at Max as if she suspected he'd lost his marbles. 'From all the panic, I thought at the very least she'd developed measles. It's been going around. How old is she, anyway?'

Max beamed back at her and announced in the same grandiose manner, 'A mere *ten months*!'

Rolling her eyes to the ceiling, Helena muttered tersely, 'What's all the fuss? It's about time. Some babies are already walking at this age.'

Gemma found herself watching this little exchange with interest. From the way Max's face closed up, she could tell that he was miffed by Helena's snub and Helena was clearly much less impressed by his interest in Mollie than she had seemed when she'd telephoned after his trip to town. Had there been a lover's tiff?

'I'd say our clever little girl needs rescuing,' she said quickly, stepping forward and lifting Mollie out of the cot. 'She's learned to pull herself up, but I don't think she knows how to let go again yet, and she definitely needs a nappy change.'

'And you need to go back to the tent and get properly dressed,' Helena told Max, taking in the details of his exposed muscles and unshaven jaw with a puzzling, displeased frown.

As Helena turned away and drifted back down the verandah, Gemma set about changing Mollie. Then she took her down to the roomy Mungulla kitchen to fix her some breakfast.

By the time she emerged into the garden to join in the adults' breakfast, guests were making their selections from the mountain of food spread beside the barbecue. Crispy homemade sausages shared pride of place beside fried eggs, onions, tomatoes and mushrooms as well as baskets of freshly baked damper and a choice of bush honey, golden syrup or mango jam to spread on it. And, of course, there was plenty of good strong billy tea to wash it down.

Max had already piled his plate and offered to take Mollie while he ate picnic-style under one of the shady wattles. As he sat cross-legged, the baby happily practised her new standing skills, one hand gripping his jeans tightly. In her other chubby fist she clutched a wedge of his damper, which she was allowing a cheeky magpie to peck at.

Helena, looking immaculate in a neatly pressed white linen shirt and slacks, moved next to Gemma and Simon as they loaded their plates.

'You slept well?' she asked them solicitously.

Gemma's eyes flicked to her right to meet Helena's steady gaze. 'Not so well as you did, I'm sure. The ground was rather lumpy.'

'It was a warm night,' Helena responded. 'Must have been a little close in the tent.'

Gemma concentrated hard on spearing a juicy sausage. Helena's unexpected concern made her edgy.

'Oh, we weren't in the tent,' Simon hastily intervened. He shook his head. 'I can't understand why Australians love to abandon perfectly good tents to sleep out in the open.'

Helena's impeccable eyebrows rose as she stared at Gemma. 'So you and Max were outside, then?'

'And Simon, of course,' Gemma added.

'One big happy family,' Simon elaborated dryly.

'Oh, I see. The three of you.' Helena seemed extraordinarily delighted by this news and her reaction puzzled Gemma some more. What on earth did the other woman think had been happening down in the tents?

When they all settled to eat their breakfast, Helena seemed much more relaxed and prepared to take a renewed interest in Mollie's feats, but there was a tangible air of tension between Max and Simon.

It seemed to Gemma, as she munched on her tasty sausage, that the men had been involved in some kind of argument while she'd been giving Mollie her breakfast. Last week they'd carried on as if they were great mates—the best horse-breaking team in the state—and now they could barely speak to each other.

And the situation hadn't improved by the time they'd finished eating, thanked their hosts and made their farewells before rattling back along the track from Mungulla to Goodbye Creek. It was a solemn and silent journey. Perhaps they were just tired, Gemma decided, but the tension was still there. Nobody seemed interested in talking.

Occasionally, when another car passed in the opposite direction, Max would raise a finger or two, or perhaps his entire hand from the steering wheel.

Gemma whispered to Simon, 'That's known as the *outback salute*. Watch how many fingers he raises and you'll be able to gauge how well he knows the other driver.'

But Max glared at her so fiercely that she and Simon

exchanged guilty looks and reverted to uncomfortable silence.

As if in sympathy with their bleak mood, storm clouds gathered ahead of them like huge black and purple bruises. But while weather would usually be a subject of intense discussion for people who worked the land, they all stared through the dusty windscreen at the threatening storm but no one commented. They were wrapped in their own grim thoughts.

The skies opened before they reached home, turning the dirt road to slippery red mud in a matter of minutes. They dropped Simon off at the ringers' hut and after a muttered, businesslike exchange between the jackaroo and Max, they drove on to the homestead. When they clambered out of the car, Max tried to protect Mollie by holding her inside his shirt, but the heavy rain poured straight through the fine cotton.

'I'll dry her off quickly,' Gemma offered when they hurried inside. In no time, she had fetched a thick, fluffy towel and rubbed Mollie warm and dry. She changed her into fresh clean clothes.

Max stepped into the room. His gaze took in Gemma's wet hair and saturated T-shirt and skirt. The temperature had dropped with the rain and she was shivering slightly. 'You need a warm shower,' he said softly.

'I do indeed.' She looked down and was embarrassed to discover how thoroughly transparent her white shirt was now that it was wet. 'I look like Sharon Foster.'

His face broke into a slow, sexy smile. 'Not a chance, Gemma.'

She bit her lip. Of course her curves were nowhere near as magnificent as Sharon's.

'Off you go,' he urged. 'I'll keep an eye on Mollie.'

When she emerged from her shower, dressed in jeans

and a red gingham shirt with her hair towelled dry into
a cap of wispy curls, Gemma found Max with Mollie
on his lap, sitting at the computer in his study. He looked
up at her and his face was flooded with joy. 'There's an
e-mail message from Isobel. She and Dave are on their
way home.' His mouth curved into an enormous grin.

She'd never seen him look like that. Excited, relieved.
He looked even happier than he had this morning over
Mollie's accomplishments.

His enthusiasm was infectious. 'That's wonderful!'
she cried. 'Mollie, Mummy and Daddy are coming
home!' She turned back to Max. 'I take it Dave's OK?'

'As far as I can tell he's fine. Isobel hasn't given too
many details. Have a look at her message for yourself.'

Over his bare shoulder, Gemma peered at the computer screen.

Hi Max and Gem,

*Great news, guys. Dave has been released. I actu-
ally got to touch him and hold him this morning.
You've absolutely no idea how happy I am. We're
flying out tomorrow! And we'll be with you guys the
day after.*

Can't wait to get home to see our little Cuddlepie.

*We owe you two so much. Please give Mollie heaps
of hugs and kisses and, hey, hug each other, too.
You're both angels.*

Much love,

*Bel, who is heading off to buy Dave some shaving
gear. My face is scratched to bits already!*

'I'm so happy for them,' she breathed.
Max reached for her hand and gave it a gentle

squeeze. 'I've given Mollie her hug.'

She stared at him, her heart jumping. *Oh, and now you'd like yours?* she tried to ask, but no words would emerge.

It should have been so easy to step towards him and give him a swift friendly hug. Except Gemma knew that, from her point of view, the minute she put her arms around Max all thoughts of friendship would fly out the window.

So instead of offering a casual reply, she stood there tongue-tied and pretended she didn't know what he was implying.

The expectant light in Max's eyes died. He dropped her hand. 'You should be extra pleased. This means your ordeal's over, Gemma. In a couple of days you'll be free to go back to Brisbane.'

CHAPTER EIGHT

DISAPPOINTMENT spiked Gemma's chest. Only a short time ago she would have been glad to escape, but now, even if she ignored the confusing jumble of feelings she had for Max, the thought of leaving Goodbye Creek so soon filled her with despair.

How awful to feel a sense of destiny and connection to this place when, in reality, she didn't belong here any more than Simon, the Pommy Jackaroo.

Max was watching her thoughtfully. 'That's what you want, isn't it? To get back to Brisbane as fast as you can?'

She had to press her fingers into the top of his desk to stop their tremble. 'Actually—I—I've been thinking I might be able to drum up a bit of work out here.'

He shook his head as if he hadn't heard her correctly. 'Station work?' he asked cautiously.

'No, something along the lines of what I do in the city—events co-ordination, promotions—that sort of thing.'

The idea, that had been sitting in the back of Gemma's head for days now, was so vague and nebulous she felt silly speaking about it.

Max popped Mollie on the floor and she crawled off eagerly to investigate the sand-filled door stopper. He straightened slowly and frowned at Gemma. 'What on earth are you going to find out here that you could promote to the public? Fresh air?'

'I've been thinking about the township,' she said hesitantly. 'When I was shopping the other day, I was shocked by how badly Goodbye Creek's gone downhill in the past few years. So many people have left and no newcomers have replaced them. Max, it's practically a ghost town.'

He picked up a pen on his desk and rolled it between thumb and fingers. 'You have heard about the rural recession, haven't you?'

'Of course. I know lots of people, including my own family, have headed for the city in droves, but it seems such a pity. There are still folks who have lived out here all their lives and who want to go on staying here. This town is where they belong. And the people on the properties—like you—all need towns for decent supplies. The cities on the coast are too far away.'

'What exactly do you have in mind?'

'I haven't thought it through properly yet.' She turned away to avoid his scrutiny. It was too hard to think when she could see those piercing blue eyes fixed on her. 'But there must be a way to attract people back to Goodbye Creek.'

'Tourists?'

'They would be a start,' she said carefully. 'And if the tourists brought in money to boost the economy, more people would want to stay here. The first settlers came to the district because there was gold in the creek. Perhaps I could do some research into those times.' As she spoke, Gemma could feel her enthusiasm gaining momentum. 'There must have been bushrangers. They're colourful characters. I'm sure I could come up with some great ideas to generate fresh interest. '

Max leaned forward and placed the pen carefully on the varnished timber surface. He rested his elbow on the desk, dropped his head and kneaded the bridge of his nose. Finally he looked up at her. 'I can't believe you're serious about this.'

His rejection of her idea was so genuine, so complete, it struck her like a physical blow. The old rage she'd felt towards Max so many times in the past surged through her, but she sensed that if she threw a tantrum now she might as well kiss her fledgling project good-bye.

'Max, give me a break. I respect your understanding of the cattle industry. I'll admit you can brand and muster cattle, yard them and sell them as well as anyone— better than most. But you don't know the first thing about my line of work.'

'Fill me in.'

'What's the use?' she fired back, hands on hips. 'You would only take extraordinary delight in pointing out the error of my ways. Forget, it, Max. I should never have mentioned my idea. I said it's still in the very early stages.'

He hitched himself out of the chair and stood before her, feet planted wide apart and shoulders back, his face a grim challenge. 'Does your interest in staying out here have anything to do with a young gentleman from England?'

Whoosh! Gemma exhaled air with the speed of a punctured tyre. She gaped at Max. His question had caught her totally unprepared. Did he really care if she had a special interest in Simon, or was he simply playing his favourite game—finding ways to annoy her and boss her around?

She folded her arms across her chest and tapped a foot as her mind whirred in a frantic effort to come up with a suitable answer. Blast him! Why should she lay her cards on the table when she had absolutely no idea what games he was playing in *his* private life?

She would leave Max guessing. 'What does my interest in Simon have to do with you?'

His face tightened. 'I happen to be his current employer.'

'Surely that doesn't give you the right to know about his—um—personal affairs.'

'But I happen to have information that could make you change your mind about staying.'

Gemma swallowed hard, totally unsure where this conversation was heading. 'How do you mean?'

'If you are planning to hang around in the hope of seeing more of our Pommy Jackaroo, you could be sadly disappointed.'

'Why?'

'He won't be here. He's heading off tomorrow to take part of the herd to my new holding up near Wild River and he'll be gone for at least three weeks.'

'Wild River!' Her anger had been simmering. Now it boiled over. Gemma could see in a flash that Max was deliberately sending Simon north to get him away from her. He'd probably given the jackaroo his marching orders before breakfast this morning. No doubt it had brought on the tension between them.

She wasn't in love with the Englishman, but that didn't matter. What mattered was that Max was interfering in her life. Acting out the nosy big brother role just as he always had.

'Why the blazes are you sending him way up there?' she shouted.

'The Wild River property needs restocking and I can't get road trains in. It's too remote.'

'But why send Simon? Why not one of the ringers?'

The question seemed to annoy him, and he scowled at her. Some emotion she couldn't read burned in his eyes. 'He'll take Squirt with him and a couple of contract musterers.'

'It's a rotten thing to do, Max.'

His mouth tightened into a grim line and his voice grew very quiet. 'So you do care for him?'

'I thought Simon was here to work with the horses. I thought he was some kind of expert,' she snapped back, knowing she had deliberately avoided answering his question.

Max looked a little flushed around the neck, but his eyes were hard as flint. 'He's a good rider. That means he'll make a good drover. And anyway, he's out here to see the countryside.' Impatience sharpened his voice. 'I'm giving him an excellent opportunity to see some more of it.'

'Sure. The most desolate and toughest territory possible.'

'It's going to be tough, but it'll be character-building.'

Her chin jutted defiantly. 'Simon doesn't need *you* to build his character. His character is quite fine already.' Her anger sent her marching across the room. She came to a halt in front of the window and stood with her back to him. When she spoke, she tossed the words over her shoulder. 'But there's someone else around here who definitely needs his character improved.'

Glaring through the window, she could see that the rain had stopped. The leaves of a hibiscus bush looked shiny and washed clean and its large scarlet flowers were heavy and drooping. The warm and musty smell of dampened earth came to her on a soft breeze. Behind her, she could hear Max's fingers drumming. A threatening, ominous beat. He was angry with her.

Too bad. She was angry with him. He had interfered in her life, scolded her and bossed her one too many times. What was sauce for the goose was most definitely sauce for the gander. She wasn't about to apologise.

But life was so unfair!

If only she could turn off her feelings. Max was the last man in the world she wanted to fall in love with, and yet it was hard to be in the same room with him without making a detailed, lingering study of the way he carried himself confidently and proudly, of the easy, untapped strength in his movements and the distracting attractiveness of his smile. And after last night it was impossible to stop her mind from revisiting old memories of his sensuous mouth, his slow, teasing hands, his devastating kisses.

Slowly she picked up Mollie's favourite toy—a stacking set of bright plastic rings—and she took it to her. 'I'm sure you're tired of pounding that doorstop,' she said to the baby girl. Without looking at Max again, she crouched down beside Mollie and began to play with her, but as she made herself comfortable on the carpet her eye was caught by the title of a book on the shelf beside her. *The Golden Years*. It was a history of gold mining in Queensland.

Curious, she picked it up and glanced cautiously at Max. 'This could have the kind of information I need.'

He was still leaning against the desk as if lost in thought and he frowned again. 'So you really meant it—about researching the district and wanting to revitalise the town single-handed?'

'I'm not so dewy-eyed that I think I can do it totally on my own.'

'But you want to stay on—after Dave and Isobel collect Mollie?'

'I don't know, Max. Perhaps it is a silly idea.'

'Now that you know Mr Fox won't be here.'

'For heaven's sake, no! Leave Simon out of it. If I had more time, or if I'd started earlier, I might have been able to find out how viable my ideas are. But as things stand, I really only have tomorrow to check things out. I can't do much in one day.'

'You could at least put out a few feelers.'

His reply startled her. 'You think it's worth it?'

'I wouldn't have a clue, Gemma. But if you've only got this afternoon and tomorrow, then you may as well make the most of the time left.'

He walked across to the bookshelf and crouched down, running a tanned finger along the spines as he scanned the titles. 'There are a few more history books here that might be useful.' Pulling a thick book from the shelf, he handed it to her. 'How about we make ourselves a sandwich lunch and then we can both spend a quiet Sunday afternoon doing a spot of research?'

Gemma got up off her knees, clutching the two books to her chest. 'You mean it, Max?'

'No. I was only joking. I'd much rather do my accounts.' He relieved her of one of the books and began to thumb through it idly. 'Of course I mean it. There's not much point in your going to town tomorrow with high-flying ideas and no facts to back them up. That's like firing blanks. You need some decent ammunition.'

They spent the most unexpectedly pleasant afternoon. Gemma had to keep pinching herself. There was no fighting, no tension between them, just a calm sense of something that felt remarkably like companionship. Outside, the rain started falling softly again, its pattering on the tin roof providing a soothing lullaby. Mollie ate her lunch and drank her milk and curled up on a cushion on the floor for an afternoon nap.

On the carpet nearby, Gemma sprawled on her side, slowly munching corned beef and tomato sauce sandwiches while she read the history books and took notes.

Max kicked off his boots and lounged in an old leather armchair also reading, his feet, in thick socks, crossed at the ankles. When he found something he thought might be of interest, he read it aloud to Gemma. They discussed its relevance and sometimes she took notes.

'I think you'll want this,' he said, sitting up straighter. 'There *was* a well-known bushranger in the district.'

'Really? I hope he has an interesting name—like Thunderbolt.'

'How does Captain Firelight sound? That's what he was known as, but I'm afraid his real name was Frederick Flagg.'

Gemma rolled onto her back, propping herself up with her elbows. 'Captain Firelight sounds OK. Yeah. It sounds good. What did he do?'

Max scanned the page. 'He was attracted here by the gold—obviously. He was the usual bush larrikin—bailed up the stage coaches when they were heading back to the coast full of gold.' He read half a page further, then looked up at her and beamed. 'Freddie Firelight was in the bar at the local pub when the troopers tried to snaffle him, but, because he'd shouted drinks for the entire bar, all the locals wanted to protect him. In a final bid for freedom, he jumped out a side window and the troopers fired shots after him. The bullets went right through the pub's wall.'

'Wow!' laughed Gemma. 'Did he get away?'

'No. Eventually they ran him down.'

'If only those bullet holes were still in the old pub

wall,' she sighed, but then she looked up at Max, her eyes bright with growing excitement. 'If we could reproduce a few authentic touches, I could convince a city TV crew that it would be worth covering a story like that.'

From his chair on the other side of the room, Max grinned at her. 'You look so pretty when you get all excited like that. Your eyes light up and you—you just glow.'

His words shocked her. And she saw a softness in his eyes that did crazy things to her chest. She could feel her heart beginning to pound hysterically and her face growing bright and hot.

Don't get fired up, she warned herself. *He just dropped a casual comment. Doesn't mean anything. Not a thing.*

But she was feeling very confused. This afternoon Max had been acting as if he'd been through some kind of metamorphosis. Like a toad turning into a prince. Converting from big brother mode to friendship—perhaps a close friendship. No lectures. No reprimands or scowls. Instead he'd showered her with warm and friendly smiles. Making her feel respected and liked.

And now this compliment…

Confused and blushing, not daring to allow herself even a shred of hope that he suddenly cared for her, Gemma glanced at her watch. 'Goodness, look at the time,' she blustered. 'We've let Mollie sleep for far too long and now we'll never get her back to sleep tonight.'

'Better wake her.' Max padded across the room in his navy blue socks and stood beside her, looking down at Mollie. 'You think she looks like a Jardine?'

Still feeling flustered by Max, Gemma pretended to study the sleeping baby carefully. Washed in late-afternoon sunlight, Mollie's golden curls, long lashes, and plump, dimpled face looked totally angelic. 'She's far too pretty to look anything like you or Dave,' she teased. 'I'm sure she must take after Isobel's side of the family. Wait a minute,' she added with an impish grin as Mollie frowned in her sleep. 'Look at that frown. Now that's a definite Jardine feature.'

'Cheeky minx.' He cuffed a feather-light brush to the side of her head and for a moment afterwards his hand lingered, as if he wanted to test the texture of her dark hair, rolling it softly between fingers and thumb.

And when his hand stayed there, just that shade too long, the impulse to lean her head into the curve of his palm was overpowering. Gemma closed her eyes as she pictured what might happen next. With just one tiny movement she could turn ever so slightly and rub her cheek against him—an innocent enough movement, like a cat wanting to be stroked.

And then she could kiss his fondling fingers...

But, of course, she didn't have the courage.

Would never have the nerve to do any such thing.

Instead, Gemma bent forward, away from his touch, and gave the sleeping baby a gentle shake. 'Time to wake up, little girl,' she murmured.

Behind her, Max straightened, yawned and stretched his arms high, as if he hadn't noticed the tension that zinged between them only seconds before. 'It's stopped raining,' he commented. 'I'll take her for a walk. I need to have a quick look around the place and check up on what the men have been up to while we've been away.'

On the floor, Mollie stirred and rolled over at top speed, her little eyes wide, instantly awake and alert, ready for action.

'Oh,' groaned Gemma. 'Wouldn't you just love to be able to wake up that easily.'

'You don't seem to have too much trouble. You were up with the birds this morning,' Max responded quickly.

Gemma shrugged the comment away. She was in no mood to expand on her own habits of sleeping and waking. Right now, she was quite certain that talking casually to Max about practices even vaguely associated with bedrooms would send her into an absolute dithering mess.

'I'll get her a clean nappy,' she muttered. After she'd returned, and had watched him change the baby with the speed of an expert, she said to him, 'While you're gone, I'll have a think about what I can cook for dinner.'

'Right you are,' agreed Max, and he sat a delighted Mollie high on his shoulders and headed out of the room, whistling 'Molly Malone' slightly off-key.

After they left, Gemma felt more confused than ever. Did she sense a slight shift in the way Max regarded her? Was it her imagination running away again? Perhaps he was still playing the big brother role. Or was he? The way he looked at her this afternoon. So sad sometimes. As if there was so much more he wanted to say. As if he was holding something back.

'You're dreaming, Gemma Brown,' she told herself. 'Concentrate on food.'

Needing a distraction, she decided to try to cook something different. Max was a surprisingly good cook, but he tended to produce rather conservative meals. Time to spice up the menu, Gemma told herself as she surveyed the pantry shelves. There was a tin of red kidney beans and another of tomato soup. She knew there was some minced beef in the fridge and capsicums growing in the vegetable garden, so she could make chilli con carne, if only Max kept chilli powder.

But his supply of herbs and spices was severely limited.

'No wonder this man is so set in his ways,' she grumbled to herself as an exhaustive search of the pantry proved fruitless. 'He doesn't have enough spice in his diet.' Setting the ingredients on the kitchen counter top, she went into the garden, wondering if an extra red capsicum could make up for the lack of chilli.

She left the house and crossed the wet grass to Max's vegetable garden and the smell of damp soil filled her nostrils. Rejuvenated by the storm and sparkling with rain drops, the plants looked fresh and thriving. But although the rain had stopped for now, the grey sky seemed to press low towards the earth like a heavy, wet blanket. The air closed around her, warm and oppressive. In the distance, thunder still rumbled, threatening another storm.

Gemma walked slowly between the dripping rows of tomatoes, lettuce, capsicums and carrots, enjoying the distillation of scents that hovered around her—the sharp tang of tomato leaves as she brushed past, the sweet crush of garlic chives beneath her feet and the earthy warmth of damp soil.

She bent to pick a beautiful, shiny red capsicum and noticed a fat grasshopper munching on a lettuce in the row behind. Lunging forward, she swiped at it and almost lost her balance. But as she dipped and swayed for a moment, she saw a little bush that had been hidden from view before.

It was covered with tiny red chillies.

'Excellent!' she cried triumphantly. And, as they were very small, she picked five. Now, when she hurried back to the kitchen, she was satisfied that she would be able to give Max a meal to remember.

Everything was simmering nicely and Gemma was boiling water for rice to accompany the meal when she heard the creak of the screen door opening. She turned, to see Simon stepping inside.

'That smells wonderful,' the Englishman said, drawing in a deep breath.

Tucking a wing of hair behind her ear, Gemma smiled at him. 'Hi, Simon.' She wondered if he had come to say goodbye. 'Would you like to join us for dinner?'

He rolled his eyes and laughed wryly. 'Thanks. But I wouldn't dare.'

She frowned. 'For heaven's sake, what do you mean?'

'Not worth upsetting the boss.'

'Good grief, why should that upset him? You're not letting Max intimidate you, are you?'

He folded his arms across his chest and his grey eyes regarded her steadily. ' I don't think it's worth rousing his temper. I'd prefer to restrict any wrestling I have to do to cattle.'

'Wrestling?' Gemma stopped stirring and rested the wooden spoon across the top of the saucepan. 'Are things that bad between you and Max?'

He shrugged. 'I think everything will be fine once I'm out of the way.'

'What on earth have you done to get in his bad books?'

His face twisted into a grim smile. 'Gemma, how can you ask?'

Fine hairs lifted on the back of her neck. 'I—I don't understand,' she replied, annoyed by the way her voice cracked.

'No, I don't think you do.' He looked down at the

wide brimmed hat in his hand and fiddled with the brim. 'Sometimes it's like that.' He sighed. 'People can't see what's right in front of their noses.'

'Simon, please!' Gemma shook her head at him. 'What are you trying to say?'

His mouth tilted into a bemused, wistful smile. 'It's not for me to say much at all, Gemma.' He touched her cheek briefly. 'Except goodbye and good luck. I'm actually looking forward to seeing the country up north— the big crocodiles and all the bird life in the Gulf. But I'll be heading home after I finish this trip to Wild River.' He moved back to the doorway. 'Perhaps I could offer just one tiny spot of advice.'

Flustered, Gemma took up the wooden spoon again and gave the meal some unnecessary pokes. She shot a sideways glance to Simon. 'I'm listening.'

'I think you're searching for your own special slice of happiness.'

She frowned at him. 'Isn't everyone?'

'Sure. But some find it closer to home than others.'

Then he turned swiftly and was gone, out through the door into the purple twilight, before she could recover enough to say goodbye.

Suddenly she felt overwhelmed, as if her emotions had been stirred as thoroughly as the chilli con carne. Gemma's eyes filled with tears. Surely Simon wasn't implying that Max could make her happy?

How could that be?

A tear rolled down her nose and was in danger of dropping into the cooking pot. She wiped it with the back of her hand. How could she be happy with a man who already had Helena, Sharon and Susan and heaven knows who else? Being part of a harem was definitely not Gemma's idea of happiness.

She sniffed away another tear that threatened to fall. What puzzled her was how Simon could possibly guess her feelings for Max. It had only been last night that she'd discovered these emotions for herself. Surely her feelings didn't show?

She covered her face with her hands. If Simon had read her heart, could Max also tell how she felt? Was her face a dead give-away?

Max's whistle just outside jolted her out of her musings. Gemma grabbed a tea towel and scrubbed at her tear streaked face only seconds before the flyscreen door swung open.

His dark hair had been whipped by the wind, so that some fell over his forehead. His cheeks and eyes were glowing. With Mollie in his arms, he looked incredibly happy—wonderful.

Oh, heaven, what could she do about this? She loved this man. And she could no longer tell whether it had happened last night, this afternoon, or perhaps a long time ago, but at some point in time her instinctive need for his physical embrace had expanded into a stronger need for so much more.

She had a sneaking feeling she was *properly* in love.

The real thing. Wanting the give and take of day to day living, yearning to share his burdens. The kind of loving that led to a lasting commitment.

A lifetime together.

She shook her head and threw back her shoulders. Enough of such nonsense. She had no chance of a life-long love with Max Jardine. She had more chance of waking in the morning to discover he'd turned into a frog!

He grinned at her. 'Mollie and I have quacked at the ducks on the dam,' he announced with a chuckle. 'And we've let the chickens out for their green pick. The dogs have been fed and—' He sniffed and looked eagerly towards the cooking pot. 'I'm famished. What's for—' Stopping mid-sentence, he stared hard at Gemma. 'What's the matter?'

She gulped. 'Nothing. I'm fine.'

'You don't look fine. You look all blotchy and red eyed, like you've been—' His eyes narrowed. 'Gemma, I saw the Pommy Jackaroo moseying over this way before. Has he been upsetting you?'

'No,' she answered hastily. 'Certainly not.'

His jaw clenched. 'And now you're heartbroken—because he's going away.'

'No, of course not. It's—it's the chillies. They made my eyes water when I cut them up.'

He frowned. 'Chillies?'

'Yes. Our dinner. Chilli con carne,' she announced proudly. 'Have you had it before?'

He eyed the cooking pot again and asked with a teasing grin, 'What is it with women and foreign tucker? First we had Sharon's beef stroganoff and now you've got this chilli con carne?'

Tossing the wooden spoon back into the pot, she glared at him, hands on hips. The last thing Gemma needed this evening was to be compared with Sharon Foster. She had absolutely no desire to be reminded that Max had a string of women. 'A varied diet is essential to a healthy body and mind and eating corned beef or steak six nights a week and roast beef on the seventh hardly amounts to variety.'

For a moment his face set into stubborn, defensive lines and Gemma expected an argument, but, to her surprise, Max dipped his head respectfully. 'I beg your pardon, Gemma. I'm sure your chilli dish is delicious. Is there time to give Mollie a quick bath before you serve up?'

'Of course,' she muttered.

And she banged things around in the kitchen as she heated Mollie's dinner and set the table for their meal. There would be no extra fuss tonight—plain thick white china and battered old cutlery and eating at the scrubbed pine kitchen table.

By the time she had things ready, Max had come back with Mollie smelling sweetly of baby powder and looking shining clean and more cherubic than ever in a fresh white nightie. Gemma couldn't help picturing him with a baby of his own, bringing her up in this home that he'd worked hard to make nice and on this land he'd worked hard to tame. It wouldn't be an easy life. His children would have to learn to work hard too and to entertain themselves. And to take the lean years with the good.

But it could be quite, quite wonderful.

She took a deep breath as he sat Mollie in her high chair in front of her bowl of beef broth and mashed vegetables. Gemma set two loaded plates on the table and took her place beside Mollie. 'Don't wait for me,' she said as she spooned some vegetables into the baby's mouth.

'Thanks. I am feeling rather peckish.'

Out of the corner of her eye, she saw Max dip his fork and take a hungry, man-sized helping of food. Then she heard his gasp and the clatter of his fork as he dropped it. Gemma watched, horrified, as he jumped to his feet, spluttering with his hand clutched to his throat. Then he dashed across the room to the sink, grabbed a glass from the dish drainer, filled it with water and gulped it down. This action was followed by another glass of water.

'Max! What's the matter?'

'Bloody hell! What the heck did you put in that?' he wheezed. 'It's lethal.'

Gemma stood and nervously crossed the kitchen. 'Are you all right?'

'I'm not sure,' he said, filling the glass for the third time.

'Perhaps those chillies were hotter than I realised.'

'Where'd you get them from?'

'Your garden.'

'*My* garden? I don't grow chillies.'

'Yes, you do.' She looked away from his glare. 'Perhaps the seeds were dropped by birds.'

'Did you taste this stuff while you were making it?'

'No. I've made it lots of times before, but I must admit I usually use dried chilli powder.' What she couldn't admit was she'd been so busy thinking about *him* that she hadn't really focused on the meal. She'd been working on automatic pilot, her mind in the clouds.

He shook his head. 'I defy any man to eat that stuff.'

Her fragile emotions, already strained to the limit, threatened to give way. 'Perhaps I could pick the chillies out?'

Max shook his head. 'Don't bother. I guess I'll have to make some more corned beef sandwiches.'

'Or get Sharon to make you a decent meal,' Gemma couldn't help shouting at him. Her lower lip trembled. 'I don't suppose *she* ever makes mistakes.'

'Don't be childish.'

Gemma closed her eyes to hold back the tears. Here she was once again, feeling immature and useless. Why did she always make a fool of herself around this man?

It seemed that although she was twenty-three he would probably never think of her as anything but an annoying, half-witted kid. No wonder he always adopted the big brother role with her.

At least he seemed to recover from his gastronomic ordeal fairly quickly. Gemma kept her mouth tightly shut as she removed the plates of food and fed Mollie while Max made a pile of sandwiches.

She was relieved that he didn't continue to tease or lecture her.

'Well, Mollie,' he said, handing her a crust to munch on, 'two more sleeps and your mum and dad will be home.'

'I suppose she remembers them,' Gemma commented.

Max's eyes widened. 'I hadn't even thought about that. Surely she won't have forgotten her mother? It hasn't been that long.'

'How do you feel about handing her back?'

He didn't answer straight away, but just sat there staring at Mollie, his jaw propped on an upturned palm. 'I can't wait for both of you to leave,' he said at last. 'You know what a reclusive old bachelor I am. It's time I had this place to myself again. It's been overrun with females.'

She wondered if he was bluffing, trying to cover how he really felt. But after tonight's effort, perhaps he meant it.

'I guess you're hoping I don't have too much success in town tomorrow,' she said. 'You won't be happy if the locals are enthusiastic about the ''Welcome to Goodbye Creek'' festival I'm planning.'

He took a long sip of tea and, when he set the mug down, his eyes held hers. 'I'll reserve my judgement till we see what tomorrow brings.'

She dropped her gaze and paid careful attention to the geometric pattern of the blue and white tablecloth. 'If people want me to go ahead with the project, I'll find somewhere to stay in town. I wouldn't want to be a bother to you.' She felt braver after she'd said that, as if she could almost believe it.

'That's fine,' he said softly.

Again, stupid tears threatened. She jumped up and began to clear the table, hoping all the time that Max might reach over and touch her, tell her he was joking and he didn't want her to go. But he didn't move and didn't speak. He simply sat staring at Mollie. Looking sad.

CHAPTER NINE

GEMMA'S day in town didn't go quite the way she'd planned.

Mid-afternoon found her slouched in a corner of the waiting room of the Goodbye Creek Police Station, hot, hungry, completely frustrated and more than a little embarrassed.

Last night's disaster with the chillies paled to insignificance beside today's effort. At least Max hadn't been there to make matters worse.

'Gemma, what's happened?'

Oh, cripes! Gemma swivelled around to find Max shoving his shoulder against the glass doors of the waiting room and dashing towards her with Mollie in his arms. He almost skidded to a halt.

'Are you all right?' He looked breathless and anxious and her heart developed a strange version of a quickstep as she jumped to her feet.

'I'm OK, Max.'

Panting, he stared at her. 'You're sure?'

'Sure I'm sure. I'm just being held for questioning.'

'What in the blazes is going on?'

'They're talking to the publican, Mick Laver, now.' She chewed her lip. 'How did you know I was here?'

As soon as he'd established that she was in one piece, Max switched from simply staring at Gemma to skewering her with his very best, no-holds-barred glare. With his free hand, he raked his hair wildly. 'I had a phone call from Susan.'

'The *post mistress*? What did she tell you?'

'She left a message to say there'd been a shooting at the pub and that the police had carted you and Mick Laver away.'

'Oh, I see.' *Good one, Susan*, Gemma muttered to herself. She could have done without the helpful intervention of another of Max's women. 'I'm sorry you had to find out like that.'

'What the hell's been happening, Gemma? Who's been shot?'

'No one's been shot.'

'No?' He was breathing deeply, as if he'd run all the miles into town, but any concern he'd shown when he'd arrived seemed to be churning into anger.

Wincing at the sight of him returning to full scowl mode, Gemma twisted her hands together nervously and struggled to find a way to calm him. 'It's a pity you've been dragged into this. But there's nothing to worry about.'

'All I want is an explanation! You come into town today to discuss a little business and the next thing I know you're heading for jail!'

'It's not that bad,' she said, trying to sound much calmer than she felt. 'Here, let me take Mollie. You look like you're about to drop her.'

Max seemed to have to drag his attention back to the baby in his arms, as if he'd forgotten her existence. 'Er—thanks,' he said, looking and sounding hassled.

'If you'll come and sit here, I'll explain what happened.'

He handed the baby to Gemma and their eyes met. She gulped. *Good grief! He looked angry enough to start hurling furniture around.* 'Don't worry,' she hastened to reassure him. 'Nobody's been hurt. It's all a storm in a teacup.'

He seemed reluctant to sit, as if he would prefer to pace the room like a caged tiger, but when Gemma returned to her seat and waited for him he eventually joined her, although he kept his hands on his thighs, clenching and unclenching them restlessly.

Mollie sneezed and Gemma searched for a tissue.

'I got the impression you'd been shot,' he snapped.

'If I'd been shot,' she told him testily, 'they would have taken me to the medical centre, not the police station.'

'I've already been there.' He jumped to his feet again and spun on his heel, striding to the far wall and back.

She concentrated very hard on wiping the baby's nose.

From the far side of the room he fumed, 'I'm waiting for a decent explanation, Gemma.'

Here he was again—acting like her big brother, or, worse still, her sergeant major. 'I'm beginning to wish I had an *indecent* explanation,' she snapped. 'If I'd done something sordid you could really have an excuse to sound off, but all I was doing was trying to help your struggling old town.'

For just a second his grim mask slipped. 'Something *sordid*, Gem? Let's not get melodramatic.'

Gemma groaned. 'If anyone is indulging in melodrama, it's you, Max. Now do you want to hear what happened, or do you want to make a spectacle of yourself?'

He looked at her sharply. 'I imagine you've created a big enough spectacle for both of us.' He approached her once more and took a seat again. In a more controlled voice he asked, 'For the last time, what happened?'

'Not a lot really,' she told him with a shaky attempt

at a smile. 'My plans started out well. I told Mick Laver at the pub about my background in promotions and my idea for a ''Welcome to Goodbye Creek'' festival and he was mad keen on the idea.' Wrapping her arms around Mollie, she held the baby closer. 'I explained to him how I wanted to promote the town and how important the pub used to be in the gold rush days. And he was totally fired up! So I went on to tell him about the shoot-out between Captain Firelight and the troopers and he was furious that he'd renovated the place and puttied up the original bullet holes. And that's when he had his brainwave.'

Max shook his head. 'Mick's famous for having bright ideas that backfire.'

'You might have warned me.'

He didn't reply to that—just waited for her to continue.

'Well, he had a ripper of an idea today. He decided to shoot some fresh bullet holes.'

'What? Through the pub wall?' Max asked incredulously.

Gemma nodded. 'Spot on. Before I could stop him, he whipped out the rifle he keeps under the counter near the till, and—Kapow! Kapow! Goodbye Creek pub has two new holes in its wall.'

'Of all the hare-brained schemes...' Max whistled through his teeth.

'I had no idea he would get so carried away,' Gemma added defensively.

'You obviously got him over-excited. What did you do? Suggest there'd be unlimited publicity, crowds of tourists clamouring for drinks at his pub? Tell him Goodbye Creek will be a boom town again?'

'*I* got him excited?' Gemma shouted in frustration. 'That's rich! You can't blame his actions on me.'

He shook his head. 'You should have taken things more slowly and you certainly shouldn't have put yourself at risk like that when—when I—when your main responsibility is Mollie.'

She sprang to her feet. 'We're supposed to be sharing the care of Mollie and I'm sure I've held up my part of the bargain. I only asked for one day.'

'Yeah. I let you out of my sight for *one* day and you end up in all this mess.'

There was only so much of this Gemma could take. 'Max, do you know what your problem is?' In her arms, Mollie coughed and let out a little whimper. Gemma forgot she was about to accuse Max of egomania and shot him a worried glance. 'Do you think she's getting a cold? She did get soaked through in that storm yesterday.'

He frowned and looked a touch shamefaced. 'I don't know,' he muttered. 'I think she might have been coughing a bit earlier in the day, but she's been eating well.' He touched Mollie's plump little knee. 'Don't you dare get sick on us now, possum. Your mum and dad arrive home tomorrow and we want you firing on all cylinders.' He glanced at Gemma again. 'If there's no real problem here, why all the fuss? Why are you still being held ?'

Gemma shrugged and rolled her eyes. 'There's a police inspector in town and he made the local sergeant extra nervous. When they heard the shots, they both came bursting into the pub with their pistols drawn.'

'Sounds like everybody's been over-reacting,' Max replied.

'*Especially you!*' Gemma retorted, but at that moment Mollie whimpered and gave another little cough and suddenly she was more worried about the baby than Max. 'Perhaps you'd better take Mollie home again. I'll be back as soon as I can.'

Max studied Mollie, and on cue she offered him one of her sunshiny smiles. 'She doesn't look too bad,' he said. 'I'd like to speak to Dan Kelly first, just to know there won't be any problems.'

'Max, won't you ever learn to trust me to sort out my own life?'

What a dangerous question! Gemma was glad that before he could answer a door in the opposite wall opened and a uniformed man and Mick Laver, the publican, came out.

The policeman nodded at Max. 'She's free to go,' he said straight away. 'We've sorted out this scallywag and don't plan to press any charges.'

About time! thought Gemma, just a little miffed that the sergeant was talking about her to Max as if she were a minor. She'd wasted the best part of the afternoon sweating it out in this grimy, boring waiting room and she hadn't made it even halfway through the list of things she'd hoped to achieve today.

But Max was shaking the sergeant's hand, smiling and thanking him as if the man had done him a good turn. He turned to Gemma. 'Let's go. Do you want to bring Mollie home with you? Your vehicle has the proper seat for her.'

Gemma frowned. 'I'd been hoping to stay in town a bit longer. There are still a lot of people I need to talk to.'

Sergeant Kelly squinted at her while he pushed his police cap to the back of his head and scratched his grey curly hair. 'You'll be making sure the little baby travels in the regulation safety seat, won't you, Miss Brown?'

Gemma smiled sweetly at him. 'Of course, sergeant.' She could argue this one with Max when they got outside.

Mollie coughed again and the cough had a raspy edge to it. Gemma felt faint stirrings of alarm. 'I'll come now,' she decided quickly. 'The Goodbye Creek Festival is not as important as our little girl.'

As she rattled through the bush on the trip home, Gemma toyed with the notion that Max had been so angry because he cared about her. It was a comforting thought—but not something she could dwell on. She was growing more worried about Mollie. Her coughs were getting worse and she seemed fretful—quite unlike her usually sunny self. The very last thing she wanted was for Isobel and Dave to come home, eager to see their little daughter, and to find her sick. Until now the babysitting project had gone so well!

Clutching the steering wheel, Gemma felt Mollie's forehead with her free hand. She didn't feel hot. Surely that was a good sign? Suddenly, she felt totally inadequate again. Caring for a healthy baby was one thing, but what did she do if Mollie got sick?

When they returned home, Max's reaction, as soon as he heard Mollie's worsening cough, was to ring Helena at the medical centre straight away, but she was out on an urgent call.

'I guess we'll just have to keep her comfortable,' suggested Gemma. 'Do you have any eucalyptus oil? We could rub her chest with it.'

Max fetched the oil, while Gemma changed Mollie into her nightgown. Together they stared down at the baby lying on the change table, looking so frighteningly quiet as Gemma rubbed her little chest. Although she didn't look ill, there was none of her usual bounce, no chuckles when Gemma gave her ribs a tickle.

Together they fed her, rocked her and put her to bed and, to their dismay, Mollie went to sleep quickly, as if she were quite exhausted. They looked at each other, their eyes wide with despair.

'Now what do we do?' Gemma asked Max, as he stood at the end of the cot with a clean nappy draped over one shoulder and Mollie's empty bottle in his hand. 'Watch over her?'

'Perhaps all she needs is a good night's sleep,' he suggested. But he looked wretched with worry. 'We should get ourselves something to eat and then we can check on her again.'

They ate a scratch meal in the kitchen. In silence. Instead of chatting eagerly about Isobel and Dave's arrival in the morning, they both avoided the subject, just as they avoided any further discussion of her disastrous day in town. Gemma was concentrating on Mollie, willing her to get better quickly. Halfway through the meal, Max got up and turned the radio on, as if he needed to be distracted from his own thoughts, and they continued eating while listening to a summary of a cricket test match between England and Australia, but neither took much notice of the score.

While Gemma dished out their second course of cheese and crackers with the fresh grapes she'd bought in town, Max went back to Mollie's room to check her again. He returned looking sombre and sat down heavily. 'She's still asleep, but I'm afraid the coughing hasn't stopped.'

He looked so miserable that Gemma felt the urge to cheer him up. The radio wasn't helping. The cricket broadcast had finished and a symphony orchestra had begun to play something sad and slow. 'We mustn't sit here being morbid,' she cajoled. 'Surely we can do something to lift our spirits—but I'm hopeless at telling jokes. I can never remember the punch line. Um—perhaps we could try a game of I Spy?'

His eyes widened. 'I Spy?' Putting down the cheese knife, Max propped his chin in one hand and frowned, as if giving the matter careful thought. Finally he favoured her with a slow grin and his eyes danced with tolerant amusement. 'And what exactly do you spy, Gemma?'

Feeling very tense, and just a little ridiculous, she began self-consciously to recite the childish chant. 'I spy with my little eye—' She paused and looked around the kitchen, hunting for something interesting. 'Something beginning with *s*.'

'Spider?' he suggested quickly.

'Where?' Gemma jumped out of her chair and scanned the room frantically. Spiders were the one form of wildlife she hated. But she it didn't take her long to realise that she'd been tricked. 'Play fair, Max,' she warned as she sat down again. 'There aren't any spiders.'

'OK.' He grinned. 'I'll try again. Something beginning with *s*.' He glanced at the dresser and a photograph taken of his grandfather during the war. 'Could it be soldier?'

Her fist thumped the table top. 'You must be a mind-reader.'

'Didn't you know I read minds as a sideline?' As he said this, Max rose to his feet slowly and moved around the corner of the table to her. His eyes were no longer smiling, but fixed steadily on hers. He reached for her hand. 'How about you, Gem? Can you read minds? Tell me what I am thinking about.'

Instinctively, she knew that he wanted to kiss her, but for the life of her she couldn't answer him. Her chest swelled with a rush of emotion as she allowed him to pull her out of her chair. They stood together, their gazes locked, their eyes asking silent questions.

And offering silent answers.

He cradled her close. Then lowered his face. She felt his delicious mouth moving over hers, warm and seeking, teasing her lips apart, felt his stubbled jaw graze her cheek and felt his strong hands holding her body against him.

And this time Gemma didn't panic.

She nestled closer, needing the reassurance and compassion of his arms. Understanding his anxiety about Mollie, she wanted to offer him her comfort in return.

This was a very different kiss from the one they had shared five years earlier. This time there was no urgent, desperate passion. This time Max was offering her a gift of tenderness and Gemma could feel his caring and warmth seeping into her. She had no idea kissing a man could feel so sweet—so right—like a blessing. She knew in her heart that it was good. Was meant to be.

They kissed and kissed some more, his mouth moving slowly, slowly over hers, tasting her, delving to explore her inner secrets. Sending her dizzy. Their bodies pressed closer, without haste, but showing each other, in every way they knew, that they yearned for an even closer intimacy.

A happy tear seeped from under her eyelashes and Max kissed it away. 'Little Gem,' he murmured, 'thank you for trying to cheer me up. You've no idea—'

The sound of slow hand-clapping startled them. Clap…clap…clap.

Gemma jerked her head sideways to discover Helena Roberts-Jones, leaning against the kitchen doorway. Her eyes were wide with embarrassment and a disconcerted smile twisted her mouth, distorting her usually attractive appearance. 'Well, my goodness,' she remarked, lowering her hands to her hips. 'How touching. How deeply touching.'

Stunned, Gemma stood ramrod-still, waiting for Max to release her, to say something, but he seemed as stupefied as she felt. She was aware of how moist and rosy her lips must look, but resisted the impulse to wipe her mouth with the back of her hand. It was too late to remove any evidence.

Finally Max dropped his hands to his sides and cleared his throat. 'Ah—Helena. I've been trying to reach you.'

'So I noticed.'

'No, seriously.' He stepped towards her. 'We're worried about Mollie.'

'You don't say?'

Guiltily, Gemma stood beside the kitchen table watching Max, not daring to speak.

'You can't have been too worried,' Helena told him frostily. 'I've been knocking on the front door for some time, but there was no answer, so I let myself in. If I'd been one or two minutes later, I might have really embarrassed us all.'

From Mollie's bedroom nearby came a little wail and a cough.

'That's the baby,' said Max.

'Oh, I'd never have guessed.' Helena rolled her eyes.

Max glared at her. 'Can't you be professional about this?'

She glared back. 'I was being *mega* professional, Max. I got a message that you were trying to contact me about a medical problem so, as I've been over at the Pearsons', because all four of their kids are down with the measles and the littlest one is really sick, I thought I'd call in here on my way home.'

'Thanks, Helena. We really appreciate it. I mean it. And we *are* really concerned about Mollie.'

Helena's face settled back into its mask of professional composure. 'What's the matter with her?'

'She's coughing a lot.'

'And she's listless,' Gemma added. 'But I don't think she has a fever.'

'I'd better take a look at her,' Helena said in her businesslike, matter-of-fact manner. She picked up her bag from the floor and moved towards the bedroom. Max followed. Mollie was still crying.

'Can I make you some coffee?' Gemma called after them.

'Thanks,' Helena replied grimly, and Gemma gathered up the dirty plates and cutlery from the table and carried them to the sink.

Surely Mollie couldn't have measles? There'd been a dreadful epidemic the year before. She remembered reading in the papers that children had died. Gemma's lower teeth nervously nibbled her upper lip as she switched on the kettle and spooned coffee into three mugs, placing them on a tray along with a little milk jug and sugar basin. As she poured steaming water into the mugs, her mind was completely taken up with her concern for Mollie. The Pearson children lived on the neighbouring property.

She hunted in the pantry for a packet of biscuits and wondered if Helena needed something more substantial to eat. But she found it difficult to concentrate on practicalities when her mind was focused on picturing the doctor in the bedroom examining Mollie. *What had she discovered?*

And, as well as her fear, she also had Max's kiss to think about. But that was something beautiful and precious that she must tuck away safely for now. Later she would think about it, savour it. Wonder about it. But even now, while she worried about Mollie and squirmed with embarrassment at the way Helena had caught them 'in the act', the impact of the kiss stayed with her, giving her an underlying sense of promise—like a talisman.

Finding the biscuits at last, she piled them onto a plate and carried the loaded tray through to the lounge room. Helena and Max were coming down the hall from Mollie's room, talking softly. They looked up when they saw Gemma.

'What's the verdict?' she asked nervously.

Helena tucked a stethoscope into her bag. 'I don't think there's too much to worry about,' she said. 'No measles symptoms at this stage. Her throat looks rather red, but I hesitate to prescribe antibiotics. Max and I have given her some baby painkiller. That might make her feel more comfortable.'

'Otherwise we continue as we have,' Max added, with a reassuring wink for Gemma.

Helena nodded. 'And keep in touch with me if you have more concerns.'

'I must say I'm relieved that it doesn't seem serious!' Gemma placed the tray carefully on the coffee table. 'This parenting business is nerve-racking.'

As she eased herself onto a sofa, Helena shot her a wry smirk. 'Parents are the bane of my life.'

'You look tired, Helena.' Max handed her a mug of coffee. Gemma noticed that he added milk and one sugar. He knew exactly how Helena took her coffee.

'It goes with the territory.'

'You've chosen a hard life as a rural doctor in outback Queensland,' Gemma suggested with as much sympathy as she could muster.

Taking a deep draught of her coffee, Helena shrugged. 'You're lucky to be going back to the city in a day or two.' She swung a sultry glance Max's way. 'Nobody out here has it easy. Look at our dear boy, Max. He has to be a Jack-of-all-trades. Cattlemen have to be able to do everything with little or no help—one minute they're fixing a broken-down motorbike in the middle of nowhere and next they're spaying heifers.' Her affectionate smile as she looked at him transformed her face.

Gemma felt her own smile growing a little stiff. 'You're both heroes.'

'We certainly are.' Sarcasm underscored Helena's voice as she put her coffee cup back on the tray. She pushed herself to her feet. 'But if I'm going to stay heroic I'd better make tracks.'

Max stepped forward gallantly. 'I'll see you out.'

'Thanks.' She scooped up her doctor's bag with one hand and looped her free arm through his. 'Bye, Gemma,' she called over her shoulder. 'Don't worry too much about that little baby. But I've given Max strict instructions to call me if he's at all concerned.'

Gemma offered an ineffectual wave to their retreating backs. The two walked with their heads leaning together, talking earnestly. For Gemma, it was like being back at the ball. Once again, she was struck by how good this couple looked together. Both were tall and handsome, strong characters—confident of their place in the world—*at ease with their sexuality*. They would make an excellent partnership. A perfect match.

What was a little kiss beside all that?

She stared down at her coffee. The mug was half full, but her stomach churned at the thought of drinking any more. Fifteen minutes earlier, in Max's arms, she'd been on cloud nine. Her heart had been full to bursting with happiness and—and what she'd thought was love. Max had held her so tenderly, kissed her so intimately, murmured her name...

Now, she'd come to her senses. She'd come hurtling back to earth with an almighty, heartbreaking thud. And the truth was as sharp and clear as an outback winter's morning. All that had happened this evening was that she'd joined the ranks as one of Max Jardine's women.

CHAPTER TEN

GEMMA hurried through the washing-up, while her mind boiled. She wanted to have everything done and to be out of the kitchen before Max returned. *No, she didn't!*

What if he acted indifferently, as if their kiss had never happened? *What if he wanted to continue where they'd left off?*

Her head spun. Her eyes burned.

Not for a moment did she question whether she loved Max. But when it came to his feelings for her, the questions were endless.

And they began with…what about…Helena? Sharon? Susan?

Did he kiss them as tenderly, as lovingly as he'd kissed her? Surely not.

Her mind seemed like a candy floss machine, going round and round, spinning out questions like pieces of sugary floss, only to have them dissolve as soon as she tried to catch hold of the answers.

By the time she'd washed the few dishes and wiped down the bench tops, Max had not returned. Gemma blacked out images of the two of them saying farewell outside by concentrating her thoughts on Mollie. The baby was the only member of the Jardine family she should worry about tonight. She turned out the light in the kitchen and hurried down the hall to her bedroom. By opening the French doors between hers and Mollie's rooms, she would have more chance of hearing her. And as she hastily prepared for sleep she prayed for a peaceful night and that she would find Mollie much better in the morning.

She woke with a fright, sitting bolt upright in bed, clutching the sheet and trembling in the dark with an unknown fear. Then it came to her. The horrible noise that had been haunting her dreams. A hoarse, brassy cough followed by a harsh, high-pitched wheezing sound. And then little cries.

Mollie!!

She leapt out of bed and dashed to the cot. Mollie sounded much worse. Gemma's heart crashed crazily against her ribs as she lifted the little form in its white cotton nightdress out of the cot and clasped the baby to her. Up close, the coughing and wheezing sounded horrifying. 'Oh, little girl,' Gemma whispered. 'What's happened to you? Oh, Lord! What are we going to do?'

Without a moment's hesitation, she rushed with Mollie in her arms down the hall to Max's room. He was already awake and swinging his long legs from beneath the sheets. Shuttered moonlight striped the room, showing up the deep distress in his face.

'She's worse?' was his immediate question.

Sick with fear, Gemma nodded. 'She sounds terrible, Max. I think she's having trouble breathing.'

'God, no.'

For a moment they both stood in petrified silence, listening to the dreadful barking and wheezing noises coming from Mollie.

'I'll ring Helena,' Max said immediately.

'I'll rub some more eucalyptus oil on her. It's all I can think of to do.' *Oh, Isobel,* Gemma thought as she hurried back to Mollie's room. *I'm so sorry. I've tried*

*to take care of your little girl. Oh, God! I can't bear
this!*

Mollie gave a little whimper.

'There, there, sweetheart,' Gemma crooned as she
changed the baby's nappy and rubbed her chest. 'You'll
be all right. The doctor will tell us what to do.'

She heard Max's step on the floorboards behind her.

'No luck,' he muttered with a curse. 'I can't get an
answer. I rang Helena's home number and the medical
centre. Nobody's answering. I don't know what the
hell's going on.'

'What are we going to do?' Gemma's question
emerged as a terrified whisper.

Max took a deep, agonised breath and groaned. He
looked away and crossed his arms over his bare chest.
'I haven't got a damn clue,' he muttered harshly. 'I'll
just have to keep trying to get through to someone.'

'Perhaps we could ring one of the women on another
property? Someone who's had children.'

Max grunted his disapproval. 'We don't want old
wives' tales. We want proper medical attention.' He
spun on his bare heel. 'And it's no use jumping in a
vehicle and rushing into town if Helena's not there.
She's the only doctor for two hundred kilometres. I'm
going to keep on that darn phone until I get some answers.'

With her heart thumping in terror, Gemma watched
him race back to the telephone in the kitchen, his retreating back, brown and sleek above long blue and
white striped pyjama pants. He pinned so much faith on
Helena. *Only Helena had the answers!* She pressed her
lips to Mollie's soft cheek. 'There's got to be some other
way to get help,' she whispered.

Mollie seemed less distressed in her arms, so Gemma

walked her up and down the darkened hallway. The only light came from patches of lamplight spilling through bedroom doorways. As she walked, up and down, up and down, she crooned soft songs—snippets of pop tunes, nursery rhymes, lullabies—whatever soothing bits and pieces came into her head. She had no idea what the baby thought of them, but they helped, just a little, to make Gemma feel calmer.

But the coughing and the nasty, frightening wheezing sound continued.

Gemma passed the door to the study. The curtains weren't drawn in that room and the moonlight sent its blue light tumbling through the window and across the carpet. Hoping a glimpse of the outside world and the serene bush might give her some kind of comfort, she moved into the room and crossed to the window, her bare feet cushioned by the velvet-soft carpet.

But, outside, the darkened clumps of trees and the vista of paddocks painted in pale moonshine seemed remote—unfriendly and unhelpful. She turned away quickly before useless tears could form. Now was not a time to give in to her fears. She had to be strong for Mollie. With her back to the window, she faced the rows and rows of books on the opposite wall. And they seemed to be staring back at her, voicing silent accusations.

'I wonder,' she whispered to Mollie and stepped forward. 'This library is old and extensive. I wonder if there would be such a thing as a book on baby care.' Spurred by a burst of fresh hope, she snapped on the light and squinted at the sudden brightness.

While clucking soothing noises to Mollie, her eyes hungrily raced along the titles, searching, searching... There were countless books on animal husbandry and farm management, international markets and economics, action-adventure novels and spy thrillers—the kind of collection she would expect a man like Max to have. This was useless. How could she expect him to have a book on baby care?

Deeply disappointed, she sank into Max's leather armchair, hoping against hope that any minute now he would come racing back with good news. She saw his computer sitting on the desk and thought of the last happy e-mail they'd received from Isobel. Good heavens! It was after midnight. Isobel and Dave were arriving later this very day. And to find Mollie like *this*!

She jumped to her feet again. Where was Max? She couldn't bear being alone with Mollie any longer.

As she raised her hand to flick off the light switch, she saw it. A shabby old book with a peeling paper dust jacket shoved sideways on top of some others. The word 'baby' in the title caught her eye. 'Please, please,' she whispered as she pulled the book out from where it was tightly wedged. She read the title. *Caring for your baby. The first three years.*

Trembling and anxious, Gemma lowered herself back into the armchair. She settled Mollie over one shoulder and, with a frenzied sense of desperation, read down the list of contents. There was a section on illnesses. Thank heavens!

Max burst into the room, his eyes wild and despairing. 'I finally got through to the medical centre! There's been a bad smash on the highway. Helena was called out there, of course. Now she's riding in the ambulance trying to stabilise someone in a critical condition while they travel to Mt Isa hospital.'

'She won't be able to help us?'

Max shook his head and slammed one balled fist into

the other. 'I can't believe this! Who'd live in the bush? What a disaster!' He stepped closer and uncurled his hand to cup Mollie's head. 'How's our little one?'

Gemma didn't need to answer. Mollie's distress was all too evident. She sighed. 'I'm afraid she's much the same. It's awful, Max.' She held out the book. 'But I've found this old book on childcare. I'm hoping I might find something in here to help.'

With a hopeless kind of gesture, he scowled. 'I wouldn't hold out too much hope. That looks like it came out of the Ark. It must have been Mum's or perhaps even my grandmother's. I'm going to get back on that phone and try the Flying Doctors. There's got to be someone, *somewhere* who can help us.'

This time Gemma didn't watch him go, she was too busy reading. In spite of his doubts about the book, she wanted desperately to find something helpful. She quickly reached the section on coughs and colds. Running her finger down the page, she scanned the text, looking for a description that fitted Mollie's terrible dry, barking cough and wheeze. And then she found it.

Croup. Gemma read through the section again. Yes, that had to be it. The symptoms sounded exactly like Mollie's. Feeling elated, sick and scared, she read on. The book stated, of course, to call your doctor immediately if you thought your child had croup. She felt her stomach contract. 'What else? What else?' she whispered desperately. There was a paragraph or two about cold steam humidifiers. She and Max had as much chance of finding one of them as finding the doctor in a hurry. Finally, at the bottom of the article, was a last-ditch suggestion.

Take your baby into the bathroom, close the door and run hot water in the bathtub or run a hot shower.

The heat will steam up the room. The moist air should rapidly improve the baby's breathing.

Right! Gemma jumped to her feet. This was something she could do. And it sounded safe enough, no matter what was actually wrong with Mollie. She charged out of the room and down the hall to the bathroom.

Eager for as much steam as possible, she wrapped Mollie carefully in a towel and laid her on the bath mat while she turned on the taps in both the shower and the bath. Then she sat on the floor with her back to the white tiled wall and nursed Mollie, while the bathroom began to fill up with steam.

And that was where Max found them twenty minutes later.

He banged loudly on the door. 'Gemma, are you in there?'

'Yes,' she called. 'Come in.'

He flung the door open and charged in, then came to an abrupt halt. Through the steam, he peered at her. 'I finally got through to someone at Flying Doctor Base,' he began, but stopped and dropped to his knees beside her. 'How's Mollie?'

'She's heaps better,' Gemma told him. 'She's gone to sleep and she's breathing easily again. It's amazing the way the steam's helped. Like a miracle.'

'Wow,' he replied, the word drawn out on a long sigh. He swivelled so that his back was against the wall and he slid his length down until he sat next to her. Just for a moment, he dropped his head sideways to rest on hers. 'I eventually got through to a nursing sister at the base who suggested doing exactly this. She said it should work if it wasn't a really serious case of croup.'

'I'd hate to see a serious case.' Gemma felt his head lift away again and she turned to look at him. His blue eyes were only inches from her and his body and hers were touching at the shoulders; the rest of his bare torso was a whisker's distance. She became conscious of her tongue running slowly over her lips.

'Thank goodness it worked. Thanks so much, Gem. You did all this on your own while I rushed around like a demented, headless chook.'

'I'm just so glad it worked,' she replied drowsily, her eyes mesmerised by the steamy sheen forming on his skin.

He took a deep breath and looked down at Mollie lying asleep in her arms. Her little chest rose and fell in its usual regular rhythm and her breathing seemed soft and even. Lowering his head, Max dropped a light kiss on the downy head. 'Don't frighten me like that, ever again,' he told the sleeping Mollie. Then his eyes met Gemma's.

His expression was so intense Gemma felt tiny pinpricks of tension break out on her arms and her back—all over her body. His Adam's apple moved up and down and he attempted a very wobbly smile. 'Do you think—?' he began, then cleared his throat. 'Is there any chance—?' His hand came up to touch her hair, damp from the steam-filled room.

Slowly he traced the outline of her face, the soft curve of her cheek, the rounded, perky chin. His thumb rubbed her lower lip. He seemed suddenly shy. Gemma knew that he was thinking about another kiss. She was absolutely certain she wanted to kiss him back. What was stopping him?

'Why don't you just say it, Max?'

'Say what?'

'Whatever it is you're trying so hard to get out.'

His hand rested lightly against her cheek. 'Later,' he whispered, and looked again at the sleeping Mollie. 'Now's not the right time.'

But Gemma thought this was a perfect time for getting closer to Max. She turned her face to his and lifted her lips. Every cell in her body screamed out for him to kiss her.

And, to her infinite relief, he did. Holding the sides of her face in his big hands, he kissed her deeply, daringly. With his tongue and his lips Max showed her exactly what had been left unsaid moments before and Gemma almost dropped Mollie, her body felt so limp and melting.

Between kisses, she gasped, 'I see what you mean.'

'What's that?' he asked, kissing her neck, her eyelids, her shoulder.

'Now isn't a good time. I'm either going to drop Mollie or squash her.'

'Here, let me take her.' Max lifted the sleeping baby gently out of Gemma's arms and slowly stood up. 'Do you think it would be OK to put her back to bed now?'

'Yes. I guess so.' Gemma replied, feeling lonely without his arms around her. 'She hasn't coughed for quite some time.'

He cocked his head towards the shower. 'I'd say we're about to run out of hot water anyhow. You turn off the taps and I'll take Mollie through to her room.'

In a daze of awakened desire, Gemma turned off the taps, hung up the bath towels and switched off the bathroom light. She padded down the hall to Mollie's room, but it was empty. Her room was empty, too. Puzzled, she stepped back into the hall and made her way down the passage to Max's bedroom.

He was lying on his huge bed with Mollie cradled in the crook of one arm and he sent Gemma a tummy-flipping grin as he patted the mattress on the other side of the baby. 'I've decided we should keep her with us for the rest of the night.'

'With—with *us*? You mean *me, too*? Here with you? And her?'

'I do.' He smiled. 'You have any objections?'

'Ah—I—I don't suppose so. I mean, I haven't—' Gemma gulped and stood shyly at the end of his bed, keeping her eyes lowered, unable to return his gaze. But looking downwards merely showed her the state of her nightdress. After half an hour in a steamy bathroom, the fine, pale pink cotton clung to her every curve. Self-consciously, she lifted her arms and crossed them over her chest, then took two steps forward.

Every part of her wanted to be there on the bed with Max. If he made love to her the way he kissed her, she was quite sure there could be nothing more beautiful in the whole world—but vestiges of the old fear clung. He knew so much and she knew so little... Then again, she reasoned, Max could hardly hope to ravish her if Mollie was there with them...

Hesitantly, she lowered herself onto the mattress and the three of them lay on the wide, king-sized bed with its crisp, clean, white sheets—Max and Gemma with little Mollie sleeping soundly and peacefully between them. The tiny warm body close to hers was very reassuring.

She felt his hand touch her shoulder. He began to

massage it slowly. 'Relax, Gemma. You're exhausted. You need to sleep.'

She rolled over and stared at him, wondering if she'd heard him correctly. Up close, against the pillow, he looked divine. 'You want to go to *sleep*?'

'It's what most people do at this time of night, especially when they've been through what we've just experienced and have a sick baby to care for.'

'Oh,' Gemma said softly, not sure if she was relieved or disappointed. 'Of course.'

'Did you think I was going to use innocent little Mollie as bait to lure you into my bed and then have my wicked way with you?'

'No, not really,' she lied.

He leaned closer and murmured in her ear, his voice rumbling and shockingly sexy, 'I'm sure I can find a much better way to tempt you to sleep with me, Gemma.'

She was sure he could, too. He'd put in a pretty good effort in the bathroom when he'd kissed the living daylights out of her. Just remembering sent her nerves a-tingle. But what she should get off her chest now, she decided, as she lay only a short distance from him, was a confession about how inexperienced she was in these bedroom matters.

'Max,' she said, lying stiffly, not looking at him and pulling the sheet up to her chin. She stared at the delicate blue ceiling, groping for the right words. But the perfect words wouldn't come, so there was nothing for it but to head straight to the heart of the matter. 'Do—do you know much about virgins?'

His silent response was no help at all. Gemma still couldn't bring herself to look at him. She didn't want to read his reaction to her admission. All too often in the past those blue eyes had dismissed her or mocked her.

'Did you hear me?' she asked a crack in the ceiling.

'I heard you, Gem, but I hardly know how to answer.' She sensed rather than saw him turn his head in her direction. 'Is this question intended to launch a discussion about my personal life, or a general chat about today's society, or is it perhaps scientific? Are you wanting a biological definition of virginity?'

A hot blush crept up her neck and into her cheeks. 'It—it's purely a social issue,' she said, her eyes still avoiding contact with his. 'I mean, these days, apparently many girls lose their virginity at an early age.'

'Yes,' he replied cautiously.

'But that's only *many*, Max. There is still a large group of perfectly normal, healthy and well-adjusted young women who—'

'Why on earth are we talking about this subject now, at this time of night?'

Couldn't he guess?

Perhaps not, she thought with alarm, when she remembered how she'd behaved every time Max had kissed her.

Out of the corner of her eye, she admired the play of muscles in his back as he reached over and switched off the lamp on the bedside table. Then, in the dark, she felt the mattress give as he leaned over Mollie towards her. His warm, sensuous lips brushed hers and then pressed her eyelids closed. 'Stop fretting and go to sleep, Gemma.' He kissed her mouth again—an undemanding, affectionate, goodnight kiss.

She felt amazingly relaxed, considering she was in a man's bed for the first time in her life.

'Just count yourself lucky this little angel is lying between us,' he murmured, dropping more kisses onto her bare shoulder. 'I promise you won't escape me so easily next time.'

Next time?

It was a thought that should have kept her wide awake, but as Gemma lay there, cuddled close to Mollie, with Max's dark shape nearby, a feeling of peace and a sense of rightness settled over her, and she yawned, blissfully happy. Through the dark, she whispered to him, 'So you don't mind, Max?'

'Mind what?' he mumbled sleepily.

'That I haven't…ever…' She couldn't bring herself to finish the sentence, but Max didn't help. He remained completely silent. Gemma figured the penny had dropped. He was probably shocked that the girl who'd acted like a brazen hussy in his arms at the age of eighteen was trying to claim she was still a virgin five years later.

She felt compelled to try to explain. 'Actually, the reason I've never—um—never made love has something to do with you.'

Abruptly, he rolled onto to his side and propped himself on one elbow. Through the dark, she could feel his eyes staring fiercely at her. 'Then you'd better tell me.'

'You kissed me a long time ago—that night of Dave's party, when I was eighteen.'

'Yes,' he said quietly and she could hear the tension in his voice.

. 'You spoiled me for any other man, Max.'

'Oh, God,' she heard him moan, and he flopped back onto the bed and lay staring at the ceiling, his hands clasped beneath his head.

He sounded so upset; she wished desperately that she'd never started this ridiculous conversation. They were both exhausted. She should have taken his advice and gone to sleep. Now her clumsy admission had completely spoiled the happy contentment of a few moments ago. The last thing a man like Max would want to discuss with a woman in his bed would be the details of her inexperience with men.

As if to prove her right, he rose swiftly from the bed and headed straight for the door opening onto the verandah.

'Where are you going?'

'I've got to do some thinking,' he replied gruffly. 'And I can't do it lying in bed next to you.' Then he disappeared into the night.

CHAPTER ELEVEN

TEARS streamed down Gemma's face as she lay wretchedly awake beside the soundly sleeping baby. She wanted so badly to go after Max. If only she hadn't been so desperate to off-load her confession! She'd made everything between them so much more complicated.

Complicated? She'd ruined everything!

A few hours ago, Max had been kissing her as if he thought the world was about to end! 'Just count yourself lucky this little angel is lying between us,' he'd said. 'I promise you won't escape me so easily next time.'

But then she'd made a first-class fool of herself—blaming Max for her virginity—burdening him with her hang-ups—and now there would be no next time. Tomorrow, as soon as Mollie was safely handed over to Isobel and Dave, he would bundle her onto a plane and get her out of the district as fast as he could.

Lord! When would she ever learn to play it cool? If she hadn't shot her mouth off, Max would be sleeping peacefully beside her now instead of prowling angrily through the dim, dark depths of the house.

It wasn't until the grim, grey dawn light began to creep into the room that the tears and her exhaustion took their toll and she drifted miserably off to sleep...

She woke late to find bright sunshine spinning through the slats in the timber louvers and striping the honey-toned floorboards of Max's bedroom. Yawning and stretching, she rolled over. *Mollie was gone!* Frantically, she pushed herself onto her elbows as the events of the night came back to her. With them came a new rush of fear that had her bounding out of the bed.

Where was Mollie? Was she sick again?

'Max!' she called as she raced frantically through the house. She stopped briefly in her own room to haul on shorts and a T-shirt, wondering all the time what had happened. There was no one in Mollie's room, the lounge room was empty and so was the kitchen. She stopped for a moment, clutching the back of a kitchen chair, a little out of breath and on the brink of panic.

Calm down, she ordered herself. *You managed during a crisis last night and you'll manage again.* And as her breathing steadied, so did her thoughts. *Surely Max would have woken her if there had been an emergency?* She stood frowning as she considered where to look next. Then she heard sounds coming from the verandah.

Totally unexpected sounds—like a man and a baby laughing!

Curious, Gemma stepped through the doorway onto the verandah and saw them.

Max was squatting and Mollie stood beside him, her little feet firmly gripping the bare timber floor and one chubby hand on his knee to hold her balance. She was laughing and squealing with delight as the cutest little blue heeler puppy rolled and played in a pool of sunshine at her feet.

'For heaven's sake,' Gemma cried, hurrying towards them. 'Look at her! Who would have thought she would recover like this?'

Max scooped the gurgling Mollie in one hand and the puppy in the other as he jumped to his feet. 'Gemma.' His eyes held hers and the anxiety she saw in them made the breath catch in her throat. 'I looked in earlier and found Mollie wide awake, but you were still snoring.'

'Thanks for getting her. I slept like a log,' she lied. 'What about you?'

'I was fine,' he replied unhelpfully.

He didn't look as if his night had been 'fine', Gemma thought, noting signs of exhaustion and tension in the grim set of his face and the dark smudges beneath his eyes. 'I can't believe how well Mollie looks,' she said, dropping an impulsive kiss on the baby's cheek.

'The sister at the base told me it can be like that with babies. One minute they look like they're on their last legs and the next they're up and running as if nothing was ever the matter.' He chuckled as Mollie tried to clutch the puppy's ear. 'I wonder if her parents will let her have a puppy?'

'Knowing how crazy Dave was about dogs when he was a boy, I'm sure there's a very good chance.' Gemma scratched the puppy's forehead.

So this is how it's going to be, she thought. *We both pretend those kisses last night didn't happen.*

Some things never change.

'I guess Isobel and Dave will be here shortly after lunch,' she said in the most businesslike tone she could muster. 'I'd better get their room ready.' She turned to go.

'Steady on,' intervened Max. He let the puppy scamper away to join his brothers and sisters. 'You're not doing anything of the sort until you've had breakfast.'

'I guess I *am* rather hungry,' she admitted. 'Have you eaten?'

'No, not yet.' He raised a questioning eyebrow. 'We'll break with tradition this morning and eat together?'

'Good idea,' Gemma replied, almost enjoying the thought. But a memory of the day she'd arrived and their embarrassing discussion about women's breakfasts spoiled the short burst of pleasure.

Other women had eaten breakfast with Max. But what had happened beforehand? They certainly wouldn't have given him a blow-by-blow in-depth account of their inadequacies as a lover.

'Orange juice?' Max directed his question at Gemma as he helped Mollie into her high chair.

'I guess so,' she muttered. 'I'll get it.' She filled two glasses while Max fetched a packet of baby cereal from the pantry.

'Can you look after Mollie while I cook us something? What would you like? Do you fancy bacon and eggs?'

'Thank you. It's probably what I need.'

He must have heard the wintry edge in her tone, because he swung round and stared at her hard. 'Is something the matter?'

Oh, help me! Gemma thought, feeling suddenly much worse than she had last night. *Everything's the matter! I'm in love with you and I feel terrible instead of happy. And I've made you mad with me and I don't know what to do about it!*

With hasty, nervous movements, she began to spoon Mollie's cereal into a bowl. 'Of course there's nothing the matter. Everything's just hunky-dory.'

Max stood still in the middle of the kitchen and his brow creased momentarily as he scoured tense fingers back and forth through his hair. He looked as if he wanted to say something, but must have thought better of it and turned instead to the stove.

She stirred milk into Mollie's cereal and began to feed it to her while Max fiddled with a frying pan. In spite of her misery, Gemma tormented herself by watching

his every move. She couldn't help admiring the easy roll
of his wrists as he cracked eggs and slipped them into
the sizzling pan. Couldn't help loving the way his thick,
dark hair ended in a straight line just above his collar.
And as for the way his backside neatly filled his jeans—
that was nothing short of a work of art.

'Keep your mind on the job. You're getting cereal all
over Mollie's face.' Max scowled when he caught her
staring at him.

Gemma blushed as she dabbed away the blobs on
Mollie's cheeks. 'I'm sorry,' she muttered. 'I got caught
up in my thoughts.'

With an egg flip, he transferred the crispy bacon strips
and sunny eggs from the pan to their plates, then set
them on the table. As he sat opposite Gemma, he looked
at her with a slight frown. 'Dare I ask what kind of
thoughts you're having?'

Blushing again, she picked up her glass of orange
juice. She had been thinking about the impossible—
about making love with Max, of how he would look *out*
of those jeans. Best to steer clear away from that subject.
'I was thinking it's kind of a relief that after we came
out here more or less hating each other and fighting like
we have since we were kids, that we've made a measure
of progress. We—we've ended up—less antagonistic.'

Max placed a forkful of bacon back on his plate. 'I've
never hated you, Gemma.'

The glass slipped in her hand and she quickly placed
it back on the table before she spilled juice everywhere.

'But Max—'

'I know you always thought I did,' he continued. 'And
in the end, I decided that perhaps it was best if you went
on thinking that I didn't care about you.'

'But—but when we were young?'

'And you idolised Dave? Back then I was always jealous of Dave.' Max's gaze dropped to the plate of food in front of him and he toyed with his fork.

'You were *jealous*?' Gemma squeaked.

When he looked up again, she was startled by the intense emotion his eyes revealed. 'Even when you were a skinny little kid, Gem, your perky smile and bright eyes fascinated me. But my kid brother was the funny one—the one who made you laugh. You thought everything he did was so jolly admirable and adventurous.'

She reached a trembling hand to touch his arm where it rested on the table. 'But I was frightened of you, Max. You were always scowling at Dave and me.'

'That's because I was fairly young, too, and I didn't know how to handle my emotions.'

She let out a long, astonished breath and wondered if her poor heart could possibly bear the knowledge that Max hadn't hated her for all these years. 'All this time.'

But what good was knowing this now? Maybe she and Max weren't fighting any more, but an unbridgeable gulf of tension and doubt stretched between them.

'Anyhow,' he added gruffly, as if he regretted his admission, 'I've slaved over a hot stove, so we'd better eat and get on with preparing everything for our visitors.'

All morning, as together they tidied the house and made up a spare bed, getting ready for Isobel and Dave's return, Gemma felt as tense as tightly strained fencing wire. Max was polite and friendly, but the sexy teasing, the come-to-me-baby light in his eye that had thrilled her last night, had vanished.

When Isobel and Dave arrived, she was happy to stop thinking about herself and become absorbed in the excitement of the joyful parents reuniting with their d͏ ter. She and Max grinned happily as they listened t exclamations of surprise over how Mollie had grown in just two weeks and how she could stand all by herself.

But Gemma still found it incredibly difficult to drag her eyes away from Max. She was watching all the time for his expression to soften. But the Max of old, the reserved and frowning big brother was back.

At least he sat beside her on the lounge, while they explained as gently as they could about Mollie's croup. The parents accepted this news with remarkable calm. Gemma decided that, after dealing with armed rebels, croup probably seemed like a very minor drama.

Then Isobel and Dave told them the astonishing news that they'd heard radio coverage in Brisbane of the fiasco in the Goodbye Creek pub.

'I told you we'd attract media attention,' Gemma crowed triumphantly to Max. 'You watch. This is just the start of something big for Goodbye Creek.' But her excitement at the news was tarnished by his bored response.

'It's just a flash in the pan. Nothing will come of it.'

And of course they listened attentively to Dave as he expanded on his ordeal in Somalia. He was a good storyteller and the details of his capture and imprisonment were both alarming and fascinating, but with Max sitting some distance away, his fists firmly clenched on his knees, Gemma's thoughts kept straying. She kept thinking about the way he'd kissed her and held her last night—before everything had gone wrong.

When Dave finished, Isobel leaned forward in her chair and stared at them both shrewdly. 'I'm so grateful to you guys for everything you've done for Mollie,' she said. 'But I must confess, I'm also rather disappointed. I had high hopes that I would come out here and you would have some good news for us.'

'We've shown you how close Mollie is to walking,' Gemma replied quickly.

'Yes, but I'm not talking about Mollie. I'm talking about you two. You've been living together for almost two weeks and—and—' She shook her head and fixed them with an exasperated glare. 'You're still as wary of each other as opponents in a boxing ring.'

Gemma and Max exchanged self-conscious glances.

Dave jumped up and crossed the room to give Max a hearty slap on the shoulder. 'Cheer up, big bro. Isobel tries to matchmake wherever she goes. Gemma, don't worry, we'll take you back to the civilised coast with us and we'll leave this old grouch to his Brahman bulls and his bush.'

Max stood to return his brother's back slap. 'I can always rely on my family to understand me.'

Gemma's lips stretched into a very flat smile.

Straight after dinner, a jet-lagged Isobel and Dave took Mollie off to their room. The baby's cot had been moved in there, so the little family were alone together at last.

And, once again, Gemma and Max were alone in the kitchen. Max scowled at the pile of dirty dishes. 'My next investment will be an automatic dishwasher.'

'Great idea,' Gemma muttered. 'Although once we've all gone...' Her voice trailed away, and abruptly she turned to the sink, flicked on the tap and began rinsing dinner plates.

Max put the milk jug back in the fridge. 'It seems strange not having to worry about whether Mollie has settled for the night.'

She swivelled around to look at him. 'I know what you mean. I've become quite used to thinking like a mother.'

As he recrossed the room to return the salt and pepper shakers to their spot beside the stove, he commented, 'You've been absolutely fantastic with Mollie. The perfect little mother.'

His gentle words touched her. 'I really enjoyed looking after her. And I know you did, too, Max. You were so sweet with her.' She gathered up cutlery to be washed. 'You'll make a wonderful father.'

She hadn't really expected a response, but Max was silent for so long that eventually she glanced over her shoulder towards him. He was standing rock-still in the middle of the kitchen, his shoulders hunched with tension and his hands thrust firmly in the pockets of his jeans. He looked so wretched her heart jogged a crazy little war dance in her chest.

'Max, what's the matter?' she whispered.

'Gemma, I'm so sorry.'

'Sorry?' Snatching a kitchen towel, she hastily dried her hands.

He expelled his breath on a long sigh. 'I'm sorry I frightened you so badly all those years ago. You know—the night when you thought you were kissing Dave.'

An agonising lump wedged in Gemma's throat. She tried to talk, but nothing would come out.

'Ever since then, I've had a dreadful feeling that I really messed you up,' he went on, his mouth contorted by emotion. 'And now I know the truth, I can't forgive myself.'

Gemma shook her head and tried to get rid of the pain in her throat by swallowing. Behind her, she clutched the edge of the sink. 'Please,' she managed at last. 'Please, don't torment yourself. I'm the one who should apologise.'

'For Pete's sake, you were only a kid.'

'But you didn't frighten me.'

'Of course I did,' he stormed. 'I tricked you and scared you witless. You ran away. You wouldn't talk to me—couldn't bear to face me. You even got out of the country—and—now you tell me— For crying out loud, Gemma. I can't bear to think how I've hurt you.'

She raised a shaking hand to her mouth. The remorse in his voice shocked her. And his pain was her fault. She'd let him carry so much guilt—had never let him off the hook by admitting to her share of deception. 'You've got it all wrong!' On unsteady legs, she took a step towards him. Her eyes and throat stung. 'You didn't trick me or frighten me.'

'What's that?'

'You didn't trick me.'

He stared at her, his throat moving rapidly and his eyes disbelieving.

'I knew all along that I wasn't kissing Dave.' Gemma couldn't stand the pain she saw in his face. She stepped closer and took his hand. Touching him again made her feel stronger. 'Please believe me. I'm sorry I didn't tell you ages ago, but I've always been so embarrassed by the way I behaved that night.'

'But you said I've spoiled you for other men.'

'Oh, Max, that's not because I was traumatised. It's because I've never found any other man who can make me feel the way you did.' Bravely, she lifted his hand and pressed her lips to his palm. 'Your kisses were too— too wonderful, you see. You made me feel so full of *wanting* you.' She heard the sharp intake of his breath. 'I've never been able to dredge up that kind of wanting for anyone else.'

In his eyes, as he looked down at her, she saw a savage battle between hope and disbelief. Hardly knowing where she found her courage, Gemma stood on tiptoes and kissed his shadowy jaw. 'No one can kiss the way you do, Max. And all I want is for you to kiss me like that again.'

While her heart thumped crazily, she waited for his response.

'Struth,' he whispered at last. His hands reached for her hips and grasped them firmly. 'You mean there's nothing to keep us apart?'

'Nothing I can think of.'

She could sense the dreadful tension leaving him. 'And you'd like another kiss?' Already he was teasing her again. His mouth was curving into his beautiful, slow smile and his hands were moving possessively over her bottom.

Gemma's pulses throbbed. 'I could do with another of your kisses right now.'

'I'll see what I can manage.' He glanced around the kitchen with its dirty dishes. 'Let's find somewhere more romantic. Come outside,' he said softly.

She didn't know if she could bear to wait till they travelled the short distance, but without another word he swept her effortlessly into his arms and carried her out onto the verandah. Setting her down, he looked around them. 'Now where out here were we exactly on that night?'

And for Gemma it suddenly seemed as natural as saying 'hello' to lead him across the weathered timber floor to the railing in the shadows. With a little laugh, she pushed him against a wooden post. 'You were about here.' She stood close in front of him. 'And I think I was about—'

'You hurled yourself into my arms.'

'Like this?' She threw her arms around his neck and

their eager mouths and bodies surged together. For Gemma, it was like coming home to be back in Max's arms, having his sexy lips reaching her mouth.

It was a kiss of pure seduction, starting slow and lazy and becoming bolder and more intimate until she felt fabulously dizzy and drowning.

Bursting with longing.

All she wanted was to give herself up to the wild fever his touch aroused. 'I want you so, so much,' she whispered.

'I love you, Gemma Brown.'

Oh!

For a stunned moment they stared at each other.

Gemma's heart pounded even harder than ever and her eyes welled with tears. She didn't want to cry. 'You—you do? You—*love—me?*' No, she mustn't cry. This was the happiest moment in her life. Or it would be if his understanding of love matched hers. 'What—what exactly do you mean when you talk of love, Max? Don't you also love Helena?'

'Helena?' His hands dropped to his hips and his head tipped to one side. Gemma took a cautious step away from him. In the dim light she could see that he was staring at her with an annoying, puzzled look in his eyes.

'You can't pretend you don't know what I mean.'

He shook his head. 'No, no. There's nothing between us. Please believe me.' He held out his arms to her in a gesture of innocence. 'When I first met Helena eighteen months ago, I guess something could possibly have developed, but it didn't. We've been exactly what I told you—good friends.'

'You seem so perfect together.'

He frowned. 'I don't see how you make that out. Helena's almost finished her two-year contract out here—

doing her stint of country service. She can't wait to get back to the city in a few months' time. Life stuck out on an outback property wouldn't suit her at all. No, I've been a handy social escort for her and she's been a pleasant companion. But that's all it's been. Helena's an impressive woman and a competent doctor, but she's not the woman I need.'

He reached for her and hauled her towards him again, one hand cradling the nape of her neck. 'She's not you, Gem. It's you and I who are perfect together.'

Gemma wondered if her heart would actually explode. It seemed to swell so hugely in her chest. 'It seems too good to be true.'

'It's the absolute truth.'

She felt his hand under her chin, turning her face to look at him again. 'Gemma,' he said softly, with a strange little growl in his voice, 'you're the only woman I love and you're the only woman I want to share my life with.' He pulled her hard against him and she could feel his heart pounding away, just like hers.

He buried his face in her hair and his hands moved impatiently down her back and up again, as if he needed to know and touch every part of her at once. 'God, I need you, Gem. And I need you here. I need you to stay out here and love me and grow old with me. Is there any chance you could manage that?'

'Any chance?' How could so many wonderful, impossible dreams be handed to her in an instant? With a choked cry, Gemma slipped her hands round his waist and rested her head against his shoulder. 'There's a very, *very* good chance,' she whispered.

She pulled back slightly, so that she could look up into his face. 'Max, are you really asking me to—to— *marry* you?'

'Yes,' he told her with a shy smile. 'Please marry me, Gemma.'

'Oh, my goodness! Don't let me go. My legs have gone all shaky.'

He bent quickly and scooped her up in his arms again. 'Better?' he asked.

She grinned. 'Much better, thanks.'

His lips teased and tasted hers. 'So when can I expect an answer?'

'You know the answer, don't you?'

Crossing to the stairs, Max sat on the top step and settled Gemma on his lap. 'I know I claimed to be a mind-reader last night, but tonight I'd kind of like to hear you tell me what you're thinking. My guess might be wrong.'

'Actually,' she told him, relishing the feel of his tightly stretched denim beneath her, 'I happen to be madly in love with you.' She kissed him full on the mouth with a fresh burst of daring that both surprised and thrilled her. When she paused for breath, she added excitedly, 'I thought there was no chance you'd fall in love with me and I've been so sick at the thought of going back to Brisbane to live miserably ever after.'

Hardly believing how happy she felt, she dropped her head onto his shoulder again. It was a wonderful place to be. His smooth, tanned neck was temptingly close and she couldn't resist more flirtatious kisses and nibbles.

'So what's your answer?' he murmured huskily. 'Do you want to get married and stay here in the outback with me?'

'You bet I do, Max. I love this place. Try stopping me from living here.' With a laugh, she added, 'Think of all the breakfasts we can share from now on. Here in the homestead kitchen, or perhaps down by the creek, or out on mustering camps.'

He chuckled and she raised her lips to his. Groaning softly, Max took her mouth in a kiss so sexy she felt shivery and melting, totally electrified. Her mind threw up wild ideas, and, turning in his lap, she straddled him so they could be much, much closer.

Above them, the blue-black sky was spotted with stars, like the roof of a medieval cathedral. From the horse paddock nearby came the occasional soft clip-clop of hooves and, from further away, the soft call of a curlew. And floating all around them on the summer's night air wafted the sweet heady scent of the starry white jasmine that climbed latticework on either side of the steps.

Happiness zinged through Gemma and only one thought marred the moment and brought her stomach bunching into knots. 'Max?'

'Yes, sweetheart?' He nuzzled her neck.

'You're sure you don't mind?'

'Mind what?'

'That I'm so inexperienced.'

He relaxed his close hold on her, but kept his hands on her arms, rubbing them gently. 'Would this question be a sequel to that serious little discussion you started last night about modern social trends?'

'Yes.' Gemma looked straight into his eyes, trying to read his expression.

He kissed the tip of her nose. 'You're trying to tell me that I'll be your first lover?'

'Yes. Do you mind?

'Do I *mind?*' Locking his arms around her once more, he hugged her tight. 'Oh, Gemma, how could you ask such a question? Why, darling, I feel incredibly honoured to know that I'm going to be your first and only lover.' He kissed her forehead. 'Honestly, I'm a very privileged man.'

Deliriously happy, she trailed her lips over the underside of his jaw, and scattered more cheeky little kisses up and down his neck. 'I knew I was right to wait for you,' she murmured.

His lips caressed hers. 'We've both been waiting a long time to be together.' He nipped her soft lower lip between his teeth. 'Are you interested in making up for lost time?'

Gemma's smile widened as his lips moved slowly down her throat towards her breast. 'I'm very, very interested,' she whispered, and she opened her arms to her man—the one man in the world she wanted.

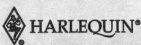

Do you like stories that get *up close* and *personal*?
Do you long to be loved *truly, madly, deeply...*?

If you're looking for emotionally intense, tantalizingly
tender love stories, stop searching and start reading

Harlequin Romance®

You'll find authors who'll leave you breathless, including:

Liz Fielding
Winner of the 2001 RITA Award for
Best Traditional Romance
(The Best Man and the Bridesmaid)

Day Leclaire
USA Today bestselling author

Leigh Michaels
Bestselling author with 30 million
copies of her books sold worldwide

Renee Roszel
USA Today bestselling author

Margaret Way
Australian star with 80 novels to her credit

Sophie Weston
A fresh British voice and a hot talent!

Don't miss their latest novels, coming soon!

If you enjoyed what you just read,
then we've got an offer you can't resist!

Take 2 bestselling
love stories FREE!
Plus get a FREE surprise gift!

Harlequin Romance®
Love affairs that last a lifetime.

HARLEQUIN Presents~
Seduction and passion guaranteed.

Harlequin® Historical
Historical Romantic Adventure.

HARLEQUIN®
Temptation.
Sassy, sexy, seductive!

HARLEQUIN SuperRomance®
Emotional, exciting, unexpected.

HARLEQUIN AMERICAN ROMANCE
Heart, home & happiness.

HARLEQUIN®
Duets™
Romantic comedy.

HARLEQUIN®
INTRIGUE®
Breathtaking romantic suspense.

HARLEQUIN® Blaze™
Red-Hot Reads.

HARLEQUIN®
Makes any time special®

Visit us at www.eHarlequin.com   HSERIES01

Families in the making!

An emotionally charged quartet from RITA Award nominee and rising star of

Harlequin Romance®
Marion Lennox

In a small Australian seaside town called Bay Beach, there's a very special orphanage—with little children each dreaming of belonging to a real family…

Bay Beach is also home to couples brought together by love for these tiny children. They're parents in the making—will they also find true love with each other?

Following on from
A CHILD IN NEED (#3650) *and*
THEIR BABY BARGAIN (#3662)

look out for:
ADOPTED: TWINS! On sale March 2002 (#3694)
THE DOCTORS' BABY On sale May 2002 (#3702)

HARLEQUIN®
Makes any time special ®